The Tomorrow People

MONSOON
MAN

The Tomorrow People

MONSOON MAN

Nigel Robinson

B■**XTREE**

First published in the UK 1995 by
BOXTREE LIMITED,
Broadwall House, 21 Broadwall, London SE1 9PL

10 9 8 7 6 5 4 3 2 1

Text based on THE TOMORROW PEOPLE, a Tetra Films Production in
Association with Thames Television Ltd and Nickelodeon.
Creator of THE TOMORROW PEOPLE – Roger Price,
Producer – Alan Horrox.

Text by Nigel Robinson, copyright © Boxtree Limited, 1995

Original script for MONSOON MAN by Lee Pressman and Grant Cathro

Back cover photographs copyright © Jane Killick.

ISBN: 0 7522 0642 7

Typeset in Galliard by SX Composing Ltd., Rayleigh, Essex
Printed and bound by Cox & Wyman, Reading, Berkshire

A CIP catalogue entry is available from the British Library.

Chapter One

He was just a normal cat-burglar, a two-bit, no-good thief with his eye always on the main chance. He didn't mean to hurt people, or totally upset their lives, but if they didn't invest in top-of-the-range, state-of-the-art security systems, then that was their look-out, wasn't it? Besides he was one of the best in the business, and in over four years of breaking and entering he hadn't been nicked by the cops once.

His main stalking grounds were Bayswater, Notting Hill and Kensington, three areas of West London where he knew the pickings could be very rich indeed. Lots of diplomats, titled nobs who wouldn't miss the odd couple of grand, lived there. Pop stars too, and even some politicians and civil servants: the burglar had heard a rumour that some of the large houses, hidden in seemingly quiet little side-streets, belonged to Her Majesty's government, and were used as grace-and-favour residences to important members of foreign powers.

This house was different, though: a large Georgian

town house set in its own private grounds and surrounded by a high brick wall. Posh, he had thought, and stinking of money, even for this wealthy area.

The burglar had had his eye on the house for days now, ever since he'd seen the trucks arriving, carrying huge wooden boxes labelled Top Secret. He had no idea what might be in those boxes, but he reckoned that whatever it was it would bring him a pretty penny. He might even come across some particularly juicy government secrets; the burglar had never been above a spot of blackmail, provided the price was right.

He looked furtively around to make sure that no one was watching him. It was a Friday night, about half past midnight. Everyone who was going out for the night had already done so, and the rest were probably all fast asleep. The tiny side-street was empty.

The burglar unravelled the length of rope he had tied around his waist, looped the end of it and threw it up, where it caught on the point of one of the spikes set in the top of the wall. He hauled himself up and stepped gingerly over the length of wire which ran along the length of the wall, making sure not to touch it. The cat-burglar chuckled: he'd sussed out straight away that the wire was electrified.

He leapt off the wall and into the grounds of the house. He briefly glanced over at the guard dogs by the main gate. They were out cold, courtesy of the drugged meat he'd slipped through the iron railings for them. Making not a sound, he slipped through the bushes and the undergrowth towards the house.

The security system was hard to miss, and the junction box was located just a little above the kitchen window. Shaking his head – wouldn't these upper-class twits ever learn? – he took a pair of pliers from the leather pouch around his waist – his very own utility belt, he liked to call it – and disconnected the alarm. The house was now defenceless.

He wrapped a piece of thick cloth, taken from his pouch, around his hand, and smashed through the window of the front door. The burglar placed his hand through the hole and for a couple of seconds his fingers flailed around in the darkness as he tried to find the latch.

Then there was a quiet *click* as he turned the lock, and he slipped into the house.

The hallway was in darkness, but that didn't matter. He was used to the dark – he did most of his work during the night, after all – and his eyes soon adjusted to the shadows. The walls were covered with posh-looking paintings, but the burglar's trained eye recognised them instantly as practically worthless imitations of old masters. They probably belonged to some American multi-millionaire with more money than taste, he guessed. Not that he had anything against American multi-millionaires, of course. He'd once tea-leafed a particularly valuable

Van Gogh from a doddery old oil millionaire who had thought that it was a cheap imitation rather than the real thing and hadn't bothered to protect it or insure it.

A light shone suddenly in the darkness, beaming out from a half-open door, and the burglar pressed himself against the wall. For long minutes he stayed absolutely motionless, his mind racing. Only two people lived in the house, he knew, and he had seen them both leave over an hour before. Had they returned?

The minutes of anxiety passed, and the cat-burglar chuckled softly to himself. He was only twenty-four and he was getting jumpy in his old age. The light was obviously on some kind of time-switch, designed to fool people into thinking that the room was occupied. He crept towards the source of the light and creaked open the door to the room beyond.

It was a large room down a few stone steps, about the size of an average restaurant, and apart from what looked like a satellite photograph of Europe (the sort of thing he saw the weather forecasters on the telly stand in front of), the walls were bare. At the far end of the room there was a large mullioned window, through which the full moon shone.

Dotted about the laboratory – for that was what the burglar had decided this place was – were countless large objects, all covered with dustsheets and grouped in a large semi-circle. It was from these objects that the light was coming, shining with an unearthly brilliance through the dustsheets.

The burglar pulled the sheet off the nearest object to reveal a bank of about ten computers, similar to those he'd nicked a couple of months before. He'd played computer games on those little beauties, but these, he could see, served a very different purpose. Their screens were filled up with the sort of gobble-dygook he knew he'd never be able to understand. He peered down to look at one more closely and read the on-screen words.

> AUTOMATIC METEOROLOGICAL
   PRIMARY TEST RUN INITIATED
> LEVEL ONE
> EXTREME CAUTION ADVISED
> RUNNING

The cat-burglar turned away. He'd never been able to understand this scientific stuff; his speciality was works of art and antique jewellery. He walked over to another object and pulled the cover off it.

It reminded him a little of one of those big movie camera lights he'd seen recently on the set of a film – when he'd nicked the leading lady's diamond neck-lace. At a little over eight feet it was about the same height, but instead of a light there was a kind of saucer attachment, similar to a satellite dish. A large nozzle protruded from its centre. Suddenly the object burst into life, and tiny sparks of energy crackled around the base of the nozzle.

All around him other machines started up and the entire room was filled with a sound like the first rustlings of a mighty wind. That was daft, of course, thought the cat-burglar: it was a warm and balmy night outside and there was no wind. Besides, he was inside a house. And then he wondered why his hair was being blown, as if by some supernatural breeze.

Supernatural! It's spooks! he decided, and as the sound of the wind increased he turned to run out of the room. And found that he couldn't move. It was as if his feet were frozen to the floor.

He looked down, and with terror and an utter sense of disbelief, discovered that his feet were indeed frozen to the floor. A thick layer of ice had formed around his boots, sticking him to the floor surface as surely as quick-drying cement.

The cat-burglar began to shiver and his teeth started to chatter. He ripped off his gloves – already a difficult operation as his fingers were now numb with cold – and gazed in horror at his hands: they were red and raw, covered with frostbite.

The temperature plummeted even lower. Minus ten. Minus twenty.

With an enormous effort of will, the burglar pulled his feet away from the ground. The ice cracked and shattered beneath his shoes. He tried to run, but his muscles were now aching and stiff. The noise of the wind roared in his ears, lashing the hair about his eyes, blistering his face. He wanted to scream but his lips were blue and chapped and no sound came from his throat.

Minus thirty. Minus forty.

The burglar tried to look around and discovered to his horror that his eyeballs wouldn't move.

Minus fifty. Minus fifty-five. Minus sixty.

The wind whipped itself into a frenzy, like a demon from hell let loose on the world. It threw him off his feet, and then picked him up, tossing him like a feather through the window of the lab.

Then there was an enormous clap of thunder and the burglar, his body covered with ice, smashed on to the grass outside, where he lay for long minutes, shaking and shivering.

From down the road he could hear the thudding, repetitive sound of heavy-metal music from the local concert hall. The noise was louder than usual, as the organiser of the gig had opened all the windows of the hall for extra ventilation. After all, they were in the middle of a heatwave, and this was the hottest night of the year.

Chapter Two

'Now what did you think of that?' enthused Megabyte as he and Adam walked out of the concert hall after probably the head-bangingest, funkiest and most earth-shatteringly crucial gig in the entire history of the world. The two friends had just been to see a performance of The Lower Depths, the most happening heavy metal band of the moment. Tickets had been like gold-dust and they'd only managed to get their hands on two through the intervention of Megabyte's father, General Damon.

('OK, Dad, here's the deal,' Megabyte had said when approaching his father for the tickets. 'Adam and I could teleport into the concert and get in for free. That way we'd reveal ourselves to be Tomorrow People – the future of human evolution and all that jazz – to about five hundred heavy metal headbangers. We'd be in all the tabloids tomorrow morning – and I mean in a big way like the *National Enquirer* – and every diabolical mastermind from Lady Mulvaney downwards would be on our trail again. *Or* you could use one of your government contacts and get us some complimentary tickets for the front row. Which one is it to be, dear father?')

'Pretty awesome,' Adam said, and laughed as the red-headed American twanged at an imaginary guitar and sang a few snatches of the band's latest hit in a tuneless voice.

'What do you reckon, pal?' asked Megabyte as he finished his rendition. 'Think I could make Wembley Stadium next year?'

Adam groaned. 'Only if you're going to be selling the hot-dogs,' he said.

Megabyte laughed and looked at his watch: it was a quarter to one. 'Look, I've got to go,' he said.

'Yeah, see you later Mega*star*,' Adam said sarcastically, and waved goodbye to his friend.

Megabyte lived only a few blocks away, and would be home after a brief ten minutes' walk. Adam lived considerably further away – 8,256 miles, to be precise – and would be home in little under one-and-a-half seconds.

Suddenly he felt something hit him in the back. He spun around and tensed, ready to defend himself. And then smiled and relaxed. A pretty young woman had collided into him while running into the road to hail a black cab.

'I'm sorry,' she said in a soft American accent, and cursed as she saw the taxi pull away.

'Hey, no sweat,' Adam said. 'It happens all the

time.' He looked at the girl. She was about his own age, with long dark hair, a full sensitive mouth and extraordinarily striking blue eyes. Adam automatically smoothed back his own blond hair, giving himself a mental pat on the back for having had his long locks cut into a tidier style a couple of months ago.

The girl had dropped her shoulder bag on the ground when she crashed into Adam, and he bent down to pick it up for her. Unfortunately she had the same idea too, and as they both reached down for the bag their heads banged against each other.

Adam let out a groan of pain, and then laughed. He handed her the bag.

'Thanks,' she said, and rubbed her forehead.

'It's a perfect way to end an evening of head-banging,' Adam joked, and was about to ask the girl her name and whether she'd like to share a coffee with him at the local all-night coffee-shop when another black cab pulled up at the kerb.

The girl smiled briefly at Adam – she had gorgeous white teeth, he noticed – and then piled into the cab, which drove away.

'Nice bumping into you,' Adam said sadly. The girl was quite a looker and he wouldn't have minded getting to know her better. He shrugged his shoulders philosophically and started to walk off to a secluded alleyway where he knew that he could disappear without being spotted by anyone. As he did so he noticed something on the pavement.

He bent down and picked it up: it was the girl's travel pass for the London Underground, which had obviously fallen out of her shoulder-bag. Her address was written on it – 21 Acorn Road – as well as her name: Lucy Allen.

Adam grinned. Something told him that he was going to be seeing a lot more of Lucy Allen in the next few days. And he had to admit to himself that he was quite looking forward to it.

Lucy smiled as she looked idly out of the taxi window at the streets of West London. She had had a good night at the gig by The Lower Depths, and it had been topped off very nicely if you please by meeting that cute Australian guy in the street. She wondered if she ought to have invited him for a drink at the late-night coffee shop, and then dismissed the idea from her mind. Lucy was a sensible girl and she had better things to do than moon like a silly second-grader over a boy – even if he was a bit of a hunk. Besides, tomorrow was going to be a big day for her and she needed every bit of sleep she could get.

She screamed. Running out of a darkened side-street, right towards them, was a man. She cried for the taxi-driver to slam on his brakes, and they swerved into one of the trees which lined the road. From somewhere far off she heard the barking of dogs disturbed by the noise.

Lucy leapt out of the cab and ran over to the man,

who had collapsed in the middle of the road. 'Get an ambulance, quick!' she ordered the cabbie, who immediately contacted his headquarters on the cab radio.

At first Lucy thought that the man in the road might have been a drunk, but when she turned him over she knew she was wrong.

The man's entire body was covered with flakes of ice, as though he had been trapped in a deep freezer for hours. His teeth were chattering uncontrollably and he was muttering something under his breath. Lucy leant down to listen to him, but the words he was uttering were incomprehensible. Whoever he was, and whatever he had experienced, he had clearly lost his mind.

She reached out a hand to comfort him, and then drew it back. Shards of glass were imbedded in his clothing and she had cut herself on one of them.

There was a screech of tyres and the smell of burning rubber, and an ambulance drew up, followed a few moments later by a police car. A white-coated doctor leapt out of the ambulance, ran over to the man and examined him.

The doctor shook her head in bewilderment, and looked up at the police constable who had come up to join them by the body.

'I know it sounds crazy,' she said, 'but he's suffering from severe frostbite.'

The policeman shook his head, clearly thinking

that the doctor was wrong. Whoever heard of a man getting frostbite in the middle of July when the temperature was so high that even the air-conditioning system back at the police station had conked out on them?

'I'm going to need more than that, Doc,' he said. 'Is there anything else you can tell me?'

'Glass,' she said, and picked a shard of glass out of the man's clothing.

'Glass?'

'Glass,' Lucy repeated, and took a small spiral-bound pad from her bag and started to scribble some notes down on to it. 'Is that weird or what?'

The policeman seemed to notice Lucy for the first time, and placed a hand on her shoulder. He nodded to the kerb, where the taxi-driver was watching the scene. 'You – back there,' he said gruffly.

Lucy frowned, and the policeman made her stand up from the frozen man's side and escorted her over to the kerb.

'Easy, Lieutenant!' she growled in the way she'd heard the actors do on all those late-night episodes of *NYPD Blue*. 'Whatever happened to the freedom of the Press?'

The policeman looked patronisingly down his nose at Lucy. 'Are you trying to tell me that you're a journalist?' he asked.

'I'm studying journalism at college,' Lucy said.

'Yeah, well, come back in three years when you graduate,' he said. 'Now move it!'

Lucy allowed herself to be moved along, but not before taking one final look at the man in the road. There was a story here, of that she was sure. And she was going to find out what it was.

Chapter Three

'You have just saved my life!' Lucy cried out the following morning when she opened the door of her flat to see Adam standing there holding her travel pass in his hand. 'I've been looking everywhere for that.'

She let him up the stairs of 21 Acorn Road to her first-floor flat. Adam looked around it as she busied herself getting ready for an important appointment she said she had in twelve minutes' time.

'It's a nice flat,' Adam said approvingly. He spent most of his time now living in the Tomorrow People's mother ship over eight thousand miles away on an island in the South Pacific. Sometimes he missed the normality of places like this – pop star posters on the wall, a pile of unwatched videos on top of the telly and another pile of unwashed clothes on the sofa.

'It's my big sister's,' Lucy explained. 'She's away at the moment and she said that I could stay here.' She scrambled inside her bag, checking that she had everything she needed: 'Travel card – keys – note-book – cash . . . Filofax? Oh no! Where's that Filofax of mine?'

Adam smiled and lifted up an item of dirty laundry on the sofa: the Filofax was there, sitting on top of a UCLA sweatshirt. He handed it to Lucy.

'Say, you are a pretty useful guy to have around, you know that?' she asked, and Adam felt himself blushing. 'Hey, you never did tell me your name.'

'It's Adam Newman,' said Adam, and Lucy shook his hand before dragging him out of the flat and down the stairs.

'Look, Adam, I'm going to be late,' she said, and ushered him out of the front door.

'Where are you headed?' he asked. Lucy was in such a hurry that Adam was finding it difficult to keep up with her. He resolved to start jogging again; teleporting was all very fine, but it sure made you lazy and out-of-shape.

'The *Recorder*,' she said, explaining that the *Recorder* was the name of the local West London newspaper.

'Are you a journalist?' he asked, genuinely impressed.

'I want to be,' Lucy said. 'All I need is some work experience on a local paper. That's why I've got this interview today with Les Bishop, the editor.' They turned a corner. 'Here we are!' she said, and indicated the newspaper's offices: they were indistinguishable from any other offices in the area apart from the banner bearing the paper's name which hung outside one of its third-storey windows. 'Wish me luck.'

'You won't need it,' Adam assured her. 'And once they've taken you on I'll buy you a coffee to celebrate.'

'Thanks, Adam,' Lucy said, and hightailed it into the building.

The offices of the *Recorder* were small and cramped, but Annette, the editor's assistant was tall and buxom and Lucy felt positively dowdy next to the glamorous African. Nevertheless she put a brave face on it and allowed her to lead her into Bishop's office.

Les Bishop was sitting at his desk, his in-tray piled with reports and press releases he'd probably get around to looking at sometime in the next century. Bishop was a journalist of the old school, and even at this time of the morning his hands were grubby with printer's ink and his eyes red with lack of sleep. A huge mug of steaming coffee was on his desk and he was sipping at it when Lucy was shown into the office.

'Hi, Mr Bishop,' Lucy said breezily, and sat down in the chair before the editor's desk. 'I'm Allen – Lucy Allen.'

Bishop looked up wearily, having not the slightest idea who the pretty girl in front of him was.

'Remember? I wrote to you asking you to take me on as work experience,' Lucy prompted him.

Bishop searched through the pile of letters in his in-file, vaguely remembering having received Lucy's letter. The girl had sounded promising, he recalled; what was more, she would be cheap. Finally he found her letter and glanced over it.

'I get a lot of letters like yours,' he said dismissively. 'Just give me one good reason why I should give you a job.'

'I'll give you a whole bunch of reasons, Mr Bishop!' Lucy said. She'd rehearsed her argument all last night on the way home in the taxi. She took a deep breath and went into her spiel. 'First off, I'm very, very keen: working on a newspaper is all I've ever wanted to do. And do I ever have some great ideas for stories! Here's one I've been working on for months.' She thrust a crumpled piece of paper under the long-suffering editor's nose, and he placed it in his in-tray without looking at it.

'I'm reliable,' Lucy continued. 'I'm not someone to let you down and I can do a good job. I can even do shorthand and I do typing – well, I've a friend who can teach me how to type. And with all my enthusiasm and determination I know that by following up some of my stories I can come up with a real front-page sensation that'll knock 'em dead!'

'Have you finished now?' Bishop asked sarcastically.

Lucy paused for a moment, and then nodded. 'I guess so,' she said.

Bishop let out a sincerely-felt sigh of relief. 'I'm very glad to hear it,' he said wearily. 'That was some speech.'

'Thank you.'

'I was once like you, Miss – ' he looked at Lucy's application letter to remind himself of her name – 'Miss Allen. Like you I was young, full of steam and I wanted to change the world. You know what happened?'

'No, Mr Bishop,' Lucy said, and leaned forward, eager for any valuable words of wisdom the newspaperman might have for her.

'I'll tell you what happened,' he continued. 'I found out that you had to learn to walk before you can run. You want to be a journalist and that's great, but you don't just come in off the street and start right at the top.'

'But . . .'

'Buts I do not want to hear!' Bishop told Lucy in no uncertain terms. 'Now, listen to me: Number One – I'm going to give you a chance to work on this paper – '

Lucy couldn't believe her luck. She considered planting a great big kiss of gratitude on Bishop's lips, thought better of it (especially when she saw the remains of breakfast on his lower lip), and contented herself with letting out a whoop of triumph.

Bishop grimaced. He had a hangover from the night before, when he had been out 'researching a story' with some of his mates down at the local pub, and Lucy's unbridled (and incredibly noisy) enthusiasm wasn't helping his headache one little bit.

'And Number Two – here's your first assignment,' he said, and scribbled something down on a scrap of paper which he gave to Lucy.

'You got it, boss!' Lucy said and took the piece of paper without looking at what Bishop had written on it.

'And Number Three – on your way out ask my secretary if she's got any aspirin,' he said. 'I'm going on a fishing holiday tomorrow and I want to be in a fit state to enjoy it!'

Lucy stood up and left the office, not forgetting to ask Annette for the aspirins on the way out. Adam was waiting for her outside.

'How did it go?' he asked her.

Lucy raised her fist in the air in a triumphal gesture. 'He's taken me on!'

Adam smiled and gave her a congratulatory slap on the back. 'Good on you!' he said. 'I knew you'd get the job.'

Lucy grinned and took the piece of paper Bishop had given to her out of the inside pocket of her jacket. She unfolded it.

'And this is my first assignment!' she said eagerly, and frowned as she tried to decipher Bishop's scribblings. Her face fell. 'I don't believe it! A dog show at the local church hall! He wants me to write a piece on a bunch of lousy mutts!'

Adam shrugged philosophically. 'It's a start, isn't it?' he asked.

'No way,' Lucy said contemptuously, and screwed up the piece of paper and threw it into the nearest bin. 'I've got a much better idea for a story, and this one could be a real sensation.' She started to walk smartly off to the bus-stop and Adam followed her.

'What about that celebratory cup of coffee?' he asked. 'Where are we going now?'

'I never did tell you what happened to me on the way home from the club last night, did I?' Lucy said. 'Adam, I could be on to the scoop of the century here!'

Chapter Four

While Adam and Lucy were racing off to the 'scoop of the century', Megabyte was having the blackest mood of the millennium. It had all been his little sister's fault, of course. She and his mother were supposed to go shopping for the week's provisions in the local supermarket, leaving Megabyte at home to try out the latest out-of-this-world computer game which his dad had flown in especially from the States. And then Millie, determined that he shouldn't enjoy a few innocent hours of harmless pleasure, had decided to come down with a toothache to end all toothaches, and his mother had taken her straight along to the dentist's.

Which means that yours truly here has to do the shopping, he thought miserably as he pushed the supermarket trolley along the aisles with about as much enthusiasm as a turkey at Christmas.

'Roll up! Roll up for a little taste of heaven!' announced an impossibly cheery-sounding salesman standing by a display of cereal packets. 'Colonel

Cobbs Corn Crinkles, all the way from the Good Old US of A!'

Megabyte winced. The guy was speaking with the phoniest Southern American accent he had ever heard in his life, and was dressed in a top hat and tails, both of which were adorned with the Stars and Stripes. Megabyte guessed that he was supposed to look like Uncle Sam: instead he looked like a Class-A Prize Bozo. He tried to hurry past him, but the Bozo grabbed his arm.

'Howdy, partner!' he oozed. 'Care for a Crinkle? The sunniest cereal this side of the Mississippi!'

Megabyte shook his head. 'No thanks,' he said.

'Aw, c'mon kid,' the Bozo said, his phoney accent slipping from Birmingham, Alabama, to Birmingham, West Midlands. He pushed a bowl filled with the cereal under Megabyte's nose. 'One Crinkle and you'll be begging for the entire bowl!'

Realising that he'd never get rid of the Bozo from Brum unless he tasted at least one of the golden flakes of corn, Megabyte dipped into the bowl with the spoon the guy offered him. He crunched, tasted — and then spat the cereal out of his mouth in disgust.

'They're horrible!' he cried. 'They taste like dog biscuits!' An idea suddenly came into his mind. 'I'll have two boxes.'

The Bozo looked at him strangely, but nevertheless placed two bumper boxes of Colonel Cobb's Crinkles into Megabyte's shopping trolley.

'They're for my sister,' Megabyte explained, and chuckled. That would teach Millie to get toothache and lumber him with the week's shopping. Hey, and if the crinkles didn't poison her with any luck she might break all her teeth on them!

While Megabyte was plotting to kill his little sister, or at the very least to give her severe stomach cramps for the next few days, Ami Jackson was considering the advantages of murdering her mother. Not that she'd ever go through with it, of course, but the way Mrs Jackson was behaving at the moment she was making Genghis Khan look like a positive sweetie.

'It's no good you saying that you don't want to talk about it,' Mrs Jackson went on – *and on and on and on*, thought Ami – as she parked the car, and started to take the week's shopping from out of the boot. 'We have got to talk about it!'

Ami sighed, and followed her mum out of the car and helped her with the shopping. She looked in one of the plastic carrier bags and saw two boxes of Captain Cobb's Crinkles, which Mrs Jackson had bought as an extra-special offer down at the supermarket. If she thought that she was going to eat those on her diet then she had another think coming!

'Mum, you just don't understand!' Ami protested.

'You're right there,' Mrs Jackson said. 'One minute you're my darling daughter, doing good at school, with not a care in the world, and the next thing you're telling me that you're one of the Tomorrow People!' She carried her shopping up the driveway and opened the door to the house. 'I mean, the Tomorrow People! What is that? Have you joined a rock band or something?'

'Mum, it's not like that . . .' Ami said. For the past few weeks now she had been trying to tell her mum about the changes she had been going through, but had never been able to broach the subject. After all, it's not the easiest thing in the world to tell your mother that you and your best friends are different – the next stage in human evolution.

Heck, Mrs Jackson had only got her driving licence last year! How would she feel if she suddenly discovered that her only daughter could vanish into thin air and reappear anywhere in the world in less than the twinkling of an eye? And that was without mentioning the fact that she, Adam and Megabyte could all communicate telepathically with each other, as well as being capable of probably a hundred different things that even they weren't aware of yet. Ever since she had first met Adam and Megabyte, all those months ago, she had been waiting for the right moment to tell her mother the truth. Unfortunately the right moment never seemed to come along.

'You keep running off every two minutes and mixing with weird kids I've never seen before,' Mrs Jackson nagged as she entered the house and dumped the groceries on the hallway floor.

'Adam and Megabyte aren't weird, mum,' Ami said. 'They're different, that's all. *We're* different. It's the way we are.'

'Well, it's not the way you used to be,' Mrs Jackson said.

'I know it must be hard on you, but there's nothing I can do about it,' Ami said. 'It's happened and it's something you just have to accept.'

Mrs Jackson waved an admonishing finger at her daughter. 'I don't have to accept anything,' she said sternly. 'I just want my little girl back and if that means keeping you in the house and away from your funny new friends, then so be it!'

Ami couldn't believe what she was hearing. Was her mother – the Mother from Hell, she instantly re-named her – actually grounding her and forbidding her to see Adam and Megabyte ever again?

'Mum, please listen!'

'No, Ami, I've done enough listening,' Mrs Jackson said, trying valiantly to keep her temper. 'I'm putting my foot down. Try and get this into your head: yesterday you were a Tomorrow Person and today you are not!'

Lucy looked up at the wall of the big house in the Bayswater side-street and stroked her chin thoughtfully. She pointed the main road out to Adam.

'That's where the taxi skidded off the road,' she

said. 'The man must have come from somewhere down here.'

Adam shrugged. He didn't understand why Ami was getting so upset about some apparent drunk who had nearly been run over in the road last night; all he really wanted to do was take her out for a cappuccino and get to know her better.

'Lucy, why are we doing this?' he asked.

'Adam, I am on to a real story here!' she said excitedly. 'It's the height of summer and there's this frozen guy standing about the streets in the middle of the night. Wow! Is that strange or is that strange?'

'Maybe he was an ice-cream seller who fell head-first into a big tub of tutti frutti,' he joked. 'Now that would be a scoop!'

Lucy looked at Adam, her face blank with incomprehension.

'Get it?' Adam said awkwardly. 'Scoop? Ice-cream?' He sighed. Megabyte had once told him that he should leave the jokes to him. It looked like he was right.

'Look!' said Lucy, and pointed down the road. A glazier's van was just pulling up outside the main gates of the house.

'So what?' Adam couldn't see what the young would-be journalist was getting so excited about.

'The frozen man was covered in bits of broken glass,' she told him. 'Glass – a glazier's van. Get it?'

She looked up at the high brick wall and its electrified fence. 'I've got to get in there,' she determined. 'I'm sure the secret's in that house.'

'The van doesn't prove anything,' Adam said reasonably. 'And you can't just go snooping around other people's homes.'

'No, I suppose not,' Lucy said, and Adam was surprised by the ease with which he talked Lucy out of it. What he didn't notice, however, was the sneaky twinkle in the young girl's eyes.

On her suggestion, he walked her the few blocks back to 21 Acorn Road. When they parted on the doorstep Adam took a deep breath and asked hopefully: 'What about we go and see a film tonight? I could come round and collect you . . .'

Lucy shook her head. 'That's sweet of you, but I really need an early night.'

Adam's face fell: it looked like he'd just been given the brush-off.

'But why don't you come round tomorrow about nine? We could do something together then.'

'Great!' said Adam. 'And till then no hare-brained schemes about breaking into private houses, OK?'

He waved goodbye to Lucy, moving off down the street but feeling like he was walking on air. Lucy was quite a girl – pretty, sexy and full of get-up-and-go. And who knew what might develop between them?

Lucy watched Adam through the upstairs window.

Once she was sure that he was out of sight, she grabbed her sister's expensive camera (hidden underneath a Ren and Stimpy T-shirt) and a long length of rope and ran back out of the house.

'No hare-brained schemes,' Adam had warned her.

Who was he trying to kid?!

Dusk was falling when Lucy returned to the house in Bayswater. Making sure that no one was around to spot her, she hauled herself over the wall with the rope, taking care to avoid the electrified fence.

She looked around. There was a light shining from one of the windows, a weird, cold light. The front door was open (it was a warm night) and she slipped into the house.

A strange rumbling sound was coming from behind a half-closed door at the far end of the hall. Lucy worked out that this was also the source of the strange light, and silently she tip-toed to the door and opened it. What she saw in the laboratory beyond took her breath away.

A bespectacled elderly man was standing behind a bank of computers, operating a series of controls. There was a wild, fanatical gleam in his eyes. Beside him stood another man, a little younger and thinner, with a sallow complexion. He had small beady eyes, reminding Lucy of a stoat or a weasel, and he had slicked back his jet-black hair to cover up his bald patch. Unlike the elderly man, who was dressed in a white lab coat and sensible if scruffy tweeds, this man wore a sharp-cut designer suit and highly polished crocodile shoes, which made him look like a second-rate gangster in a third-rate movie thriller. Before them were arranged, in a large semi-circle, banks of scientific instruments, the likes of which Lucy had only ever seen before in science-fiction movies. But that was nothing compared to what was suspended in the middle.

Hovering above the semi-circle, about ten feet from the ground, there was a cloud; a big black storm cloud. There was a crash of thunder and Lucy realised that that must have been the source of the rumbling noise she had heard in the hallway.

The white-suited scientist flicked another switch, and the thunder ceased; a huge bolt of lightning streaked out of the cloud and struck the ground beneath.

Lucy hid behind a bank of computers to take a better look. She reached for her camera and started taking photos of the amazing experiments going on right before her very eyes.

The scientist operated another control and flakes of snow started to fall out of the cloud. Lucy carried on clicking as he adjusted the power on his machine, and the snowfall turned into a raging blizzard. Particles of ice began to form on the equipment.

The scientist turned to his companion. 'There,

Wilkie, am I a genius or am I a genius?' he asked in a plummy upper-class English accent.

'I guess you wouldn't be picking up a million bucks just for making coffee, Professor Middlemass,' the other replied. His voice was as oily as his hair, and he spoke with a heavy Brooklyn accent.

Realising that this was probably the nearest he would ever get to a compliment from Wilkie, Middlemass deactivated his machine. Almost immediately the cloud faded away, the only evidence that it had been there a sheet of ice and a puddle of rainwater on the parquet floor.

Click.

Wilkie turned around, alerted by the noise. 'What's that?' he asked. 'It sounded like a camera. Didn't you hear nothing, smart guy?'

Middlemass shook his head and tut-tutted. 'That's a double negative, old bean,' he said disapprovingly, and corrected the man's grammar. 'It should be: "Didn't you hear something?".'

'Sure I heard something!' said Wilkie. 'Didn't you hear nothing?'

Wilkie stalked towards the bank of computers behind which Lucy was hiding. Within seconds he would discover her.

With no time to think, Lucy leapt out of hiding and ran for the door, overturning a chair on the way to impede Wilkie's progress. With a curse, Wilkie fell over the chair. It was the only delay Lucy needed, and she ran across the hall floor and out into the grounds of the house.

She had been right! A machine that could recreate any kind of weather conditions you might care to mention: it was the scoop of the century. It was essential that she get a message to Mr Bishop and drop off her film with the vital photographic evidence.

She opened the cast-iron gates and ran out into the streets of Bayswater, glancing behind her to see if she was being followed. Wilkie had vanished, and she assumed that he had given up the chase.

She had never been more wrong in her entire life.

Adam looked at his watch: it was 9.00 am precisely. He tidied up his hair once more, smoothed the crease in his chinos, and rang the doorbell of 21 Acorn Road. He was really looking forward to seeing Lucy again. There were a couple of great new movies on at the Multiplex down the road and he thought that they could have breakfast in a trendy café before taking the matinee. He just hoped she didn't want to see the new sci-fi blockbuster: he could never quite believe some of the crazy far-fetched storylines these writers came up with. The door opened.

'Hi, Lucy!' Adam smiled.

'I'm sorry?' A middle-aged man dressed in a cardigan and slippers had opened the door. 'Can I help you?'

'I'm looking for Lucy,' Adam said and frowned. He had the weirdest notion that something very strange indeed was going on here. A woman, presumably the man's wife, joined him at the door.

'Who is it?' she asked.

The man shook his head. 'I'm not sure, dear,' he said. 'This young boy here wants someone called Lucy.'

'There's no one here called Lucy,' the woman told Adam. 'Are you sure you've got the right address?'

'This is the house,' Adam insisted. 'I was here yesterday!'

'You couldn't have been,' said the man. 'My wife and I have been here for seven years now.'

'Look, her name is Lucy Allen,' Adam continued. 'She lives here with her older sister.'

So earnest did Adam appear that the couple invited him up to their – Lucy's – flat. When Adam saw the flat he turned so pale that the woman offered him a glass of water.

The flat had completely changed. There were no pop posters on the walls, no unwatched videos on the top of the TV, no dirty washing piled up untidily on the sofa. It was nothing more than the tidy and slightly quaint apartment of the middle-aged couple standing before him. It was like Lucy had never existed.

'And you say you've been here for seven years?' he asked the couple.

'That's right, dear.'

'That's impossible!' he said, but even Adam had to believe the evidence of his own eyes. Had he dreamt about coming here with Lucy the day before? Or was he going mad?

Or was there something much more sinister afoot?

Chapter Five

Ami opened the front door to see Megabyte's smiling face. She sighed, which was hardly the sort of welcome he'd been hoping for.

'I hear you do a mighty fine cup of coffee here!' he wisecracked. The smell of freshly-brewed coffee was coming from the Jacksons' kitchen. Megabyte decided it was probably one of the best smells in the entire world. When Ami didn't invite him in he said: 'Are you going to invite me in for a coffee or am I going to have to drink it through a real long straw?'

'Look, Megabyte, maybe this isn't a good idea,' Ami said, and glanced down the hallway. Her mother was just coming out of the kitchen, and when she saw Megabyte she frowned.

'OK, so the straw gag sucks, but I got plenty more!' Megabyte said, and nodded at Ami's mother. 'Hi there, Mrs Jackson. How are you doing?'

'Megabyte, it's nothing personal,' Mrs Jackson began, and Ami urged her in vain to be quiet. 'I like you and you're a nice boy but I don't want my daughter going around with you anymore.'

'Hey, Mrs Jackson – '

'It's not just you, it's Adam as well,' she continued. 'When you lot get together then it just means trouble – bad trouble.'

'Hey, if you're talking about that trouble at the hospital a few months back . . .'

'Don't even remind me of that!' Mrs Jackson said. She had been recuperating from an operation in a country hospital when Ami had first met Adam and Megabyte. She wasn't quite sure what had happened at the hospital, but there were reports of kidnappings, mad scientists and even giant killer-mosquitoes. She'd never quite got to the bottom of it when she had come out of hospital but she somehow knew that Adam and Megabyte had been involved in it.

'I don't want my Ami mixed up in this any more,' she said finally. 'I want her to live a normal life again. So goodbye, Megabyte!'

And with that she slammed the door in Megabyte's face.

'Oh well,' Megabyte said to himself. 'I guess I drink too much coffee anyway . . .'

Somewhere on an island in the South Pacific Adam sat brooding in the Tomorrow People's mother ship, that strange alien spacecraft which had been sent by an unknown race to seek out emergent telepaths and help them to realise their true potential. He was spending more and more time there nowadays, and he found that being alone in the ship helped him think.

There was a flash of light, a crackle of energy, and Megabyte appeared before him. He was scowling.

'What a way to start the day!' he complained. 'All I wanted was a cup of coffee! It wasn't like I wanted a three-course breakfast.'

He looked at Adam, who had barely acknowledged his presence. The Australian boy looked about as miserable as a wet weekend in Woolloomooloo.

'I thought I was going to be the one to come along here and be miserable,' he said. 'Guess you beat me to it! OK, forget about me and my troubles. You want to talk about it, Adam?'

Adam nodded and told him about Lucy and how she had seemingly disappeared. Megabyte was sympathetic but not overly impressed. After all, Lucy was only a girl; there were approximately one billion others like her on this planet.

'So that's it? You lost your girl?' he said. 'I'd say it's definitely a case of *cherchez la femme*, old buddy!'

Adam had the vaguest suspicion that Megabyte was making fun of him. 'It's not a laughing matter, Megabyte,' he told him.

'You must have made quite an impression on her. One day with you and she packs her bags and leaves,' he joked. 'A slight hint, maybe?'

'It wasn't even a date,' Adam said self-defensively.

'I only took her to the newspaper officer to get her interviewed – ' He leapt to his feet. 'Of course! That's it! That guy, Bishop, he might know where she is!'

'You don't give up, do you?' Megabyte said, but Adam had already disappeared, teleporting himself back to England in a burst of parapsychic energy.

'Boy, Adam, have you ever got it bad,' said Megabyte. He supposed he ought to follow him: heaven knows what sort of mess a lovestruck Adam would get into on his own!

'I'm sorry, Mister Bishop is away on a fishing holiday for a few days,' Annette said when Adam and Megabyte turned up at the offices of the *Recorder*.

'Can you tell us where he's gone?' Adam said urgently. 'It's very important that we see him.'

Annette shook her head. Mr Bishop had given instructions not to be disturbed under any circumstances, she told them. She would, however, take a message and make sure that he got it on his return. The phone rang and she excused herself, and then left the office to hand an important package over to a motorcycle courier.

As soon as she had left, Adam and Megabyte sneaked into Bishop's office and started to rifle through his files and drawers.

'This is crazy!' Adam said. 'We don't even know what we're looking for.'

'Something! Anything!' Megabyte said, and picked up a pile of folders, placing them on top of Bishop's answering machine. He accidentally switched the machine on, and the two boys froze as they heard Lucy's recorded voice play back.

'Mr Bishop, this is Lucy Allen. Look, I know I didn't follow your advice but I may be on to the story of the century. You see there's this big house and – '

Lucy screamed, and on the tape Adam and Megabyte heard the sound of a struggle. Then the line went dead.

'She's in trouble,' Adam said. 'Let's go.'

'But where?' Megabyte asked. 'We don't even know where she is!'

'The big house,' Adam said. 'I went there with her. Link your mind to mine!'

Adam whistled appreciatively at the array of futuristic equipment stored in Middlemass's lab. He'd never seen the likes of these machines before: they looked as if they'd come from an episode of *Star Trek: The Next Generation*. He wondered what their purpose was.

'This is the place,' he told Megabyte, who was examining one of the computers. 'Lucy told me she thought that there was something really weird going on here.'

'Help me! Help me! Please!'

Adam and Megabyte exchanged a worried look. 'That was Lucy's voice!' Adam told Megabyte.

'Then let's go and get her,' Megabyte said and started to run off in the direction of the voice.

And then all hell broke loose. There came a rushing sound like the howl of the wind as, one by one, the machines in the laboratory switched themselves on. Adam and Megabyte looked around in terror, but there was no time to run or to teleport out of danger. A bolt of white-hot lightning shot out, seemingly from nowhere, and struck the Tomorrow People. So great was the force of the blast that Adam and Megabyte were both lifted off their feet and slammed against the wall. They thudded to the ground, more dead than alive.

In the shadows where he had been watching them, Professor Middlemass deactivated the weather machine. He turned to his colleague.

'I didn't build the machine for this,' he said. There was a genuine note of regret in his voice.

'Shut up!' Wilkie ordered. He took from his jacket a lethal-looking syringe, and advanced on the unconscious Adam and Megabyte. 'Shut up and enjoy the fun.'

The syringe was filled with one of the most deadly poisons known to man. Within seconds of the poison being injected into their bloodstreams Adam and Megabyte would be dead. Wilkie chuckled evilly, the way the gangsters in all his favourite movies did. He was really going to enjoy this; there was nothing he liked better than a good killing.

Chapter Six

'You had no right to do that to Megabyte,' Ami angrily told her mother as she sat at the breakfast table. 'He's a friend.'

'Your best friend's your mother, and that's why I'm doing this,' Mrs Jackson stated quite categorically. She poured out a bowl of Colonel Cobb's Crinkles, and passed it to Ami. 'Now eat your cereal!'

'Yuk,' was Ami's reaction as soon as she had tasted one mouthful of the cornflakes.

Mrs Jackson glared at her daughter, convinced that she was being awkward just to spite her. 'I saw them advertised on TV,' she said, picking up a spoon. 'They're very nice . . .' She pulled a face: she'd tasted better things. 'Ami, what's wrong?'

Ami froze and her eyes glazed over. 'It's Adam and Megabyte. Something's happened to them!'

She stood up and pressed her hands to her head. She had suddenly developed a screaming headache, and all she knew was that Adam and Megabyte were about to die. She had to do something – anything – to help. But what?

Mrs Jackson was at her daughter's side in an instant. 'Ami, what is it?'

'I must help them! I must help them!' Ami kept repeating over and over again. She reached out to Adam and Megabyte, linking her conscious mind to their unconscious thoughts, giving them her strength, sharing her power with theirs.

There was an almighty crash of dishes as the Jacksons' kitchen table seemed to explode with white light. Before Mrs Jackson's astounded eyes pin-prick points of energy seemed to appear and disappear, to collide and coalesce; it was like the greatest firework display ever, and all of it taking place in her kitchen.

And then the flickering lights took on a form, or rather two forms. Suddenly Adam and Megabyte were there, lying unconscious on her own kitchen table.

She stared accusingly at Ami, who returned her mother's look with a sheepish smile.

'Er, Mum, I think there's something I've got to tell you . . .'

Wilkie was more than a little peeved. There he was, all psyched up and ready for a fun killing, and his two victims had the affrontery to vanish into thin air. He turned to Middlemass to provide some sort of explanation, but the scientist was as mystified as he was. Or if he knew something then he certainly wasn't telling.

Middlemass allowed himself the luxury of a small smile. 'It looks like you let them get away,' he said, delighted to see the slick hoodlum, whom he had never really liked, come unstuck.

Wilkie growled at him. 'You are cruising for a bruising,' he said, and handed the professor his portable phone. 'Now get the boss on the line.'

'Me? Why me?'

'Because it looks like our little caper here has been rumbled,' Wilkie said, 'and the big guy has to be told.'

Middlemass tossed the phone back to Wilkie. 'You tell him, matey,' he said. 'There's nothing pertaining to security in my job specification.'

Wilkie, who had always had trouble with words of more than one syllable, frowned. Nevertheless he punched out a thirteen-digit international number on the phone, and waited impatiently as the connection was being made.

Three and a half thousand miles across the Atlantic the phone was answered on the first ring.

'Talk to me!' The voice in the other end of the line was firm and authoritative and spoke with a Deep South accent.

'Er, those two kids, boss,' Wilkie said. 'They . . . sort of vanished.'

'What in tarnation are you telling me, boy?' Wilkie's employer shouted in a voice so loud that even Middlemass could hear it at the far end of the lab.

'Do you mean they just disappeared like two bugs down a bullfrog's gullet? You're a mutton-head, Wilkie! You make sure that you cover your tracks real good or next time we meet I'm going to whip your hide all the way from here to Albuquerque!'

Middlemass smiled ironically as Wilkie hung up. The gangster had turned as white as a sheet.

'I take it our employer is not a happy bunny?' he asked.

'We've got to get out of here,' Wilkie decided. 'You pack up your machine and I'll go get the girl.'

'Surely we're not taking her?' Middlemass asked in amazement.

'We've got to find out exactly what she knows,' Wilkie said.

'But where are we going?'

'Listen, brains, if you want to stand around here playing twenty questions until the cops come then that's your funeral. Me, I'm outta here!'

For once, Middlemass conceded that Wilkie was talking good sense. 'I'll pack up my machine,' he said, and then looked beseechingly at Wilkie. 'And when we do make our getaway try not to drive too fast, will you? I get car-sick.'

Adam groaned and opened his eyes. He was lying on the sofa in the Jacksons' front room, and Ami, Megabyte and Mrs Jackson were all looking down at him in concern.

'How long have I been out for?' he asked, and tried to stand up. He promptly fell back down on to the sofa again. His legs were still unsteady after his experience in the laboratory.

'Steady on!' Mrs Jackson advised. 'You're not Superman, you know!'

Adam made another attempt to stand up on his shaking legs. This time he had more success. 'We've got to go back and find Lucy,' he said.

'Ready when you are,' Megabyte said.

Adam looked over at Ami. 'Are you coming too?'

'No, she is not,' Mrs Jackson was firm. 'While you were out cold Ami finally told me all about the Tomorrow People and what you really are – the next stage in human evolution. I've heard about all the terrible and dangerous people you've already fought – Lady Mulvaney, Colonel Masters, Doctor Culex. And I don't want her being mixed up in that sort of thing ever again.'

Ami implored her mother; 'Mum, a girl's gone missing.'

'And it's a terrible thing,' Mrs Jackson said. 'But you are still not going!'

'Suppose it was me who was in danger?' Ami asked.

'I'd be tearing my hair out with worry,' she replied.

'And suppose there was a person who could help, someone who might be able to find me? Wouldn't you want that person to do everything they could to bring me back?'

Couldn't her mother see that they were the only people who might just be able to save Lucy? They had to try and help her, no matter what the danger was to them. After all, that was what being a Tomorrow Person was all about.

'Do you really think you could do that, darling?' Mrs Jackson said after she had had a few moments to reflect on Ami's words.

'I can try,' she said. 'We can try . . .'

With tears in her eyes Mrs Jackson hugged her daughter. 'Bring her back safely then, darling,' she said. 'And all of you – look after yourselves.'

Adam, Ami and Megabyte materialized in the grounds of the big house. Even though the sun was shining, an aura of evil still seemed to enshroud the house, and Adam cautioned care: whatever Middlemass and Wilkie were doing here they knew it was dangerous.

'And who have we here?' asked a plummy voice behind them. They all turned around to see a fat little old lady looking curiously at them. She was holding a pair of secateurs, and it was obvious that she had been doing the gardening.

'What have you done to Lucy?' Adam demanded, and was dismayed when the old lady didn't react to the name. 'You're holding Lucy Allen hostage in this house!'

'Hostage!' The old lady laughed. 'This is Bayswater, laddie, not Beirut.' She walked up to the front door and opened it for them. 'You'd better come inside. I'm sure there's a simple explanation for all this.'

'Yeah, we'd really love to hear it,' said Megabyte. 'We were nearly killed here last night.'

'How very unfortunate,' said the old lady, who introduced herself as Mrs Butterworth. She looked uncertainly at Megabyte, clearly not believing him, and wondered whether she had allowed a total nutter into her house.

'Look, lady, we know there's some kind of weird experiment taking place in your cellar,' Megabyte insisted.

By now Mrs Butterworth was convinced that Megabyte was, indeed, a total nutter. 'Young man, I have lived in this house for the last forty-five years,' she said, and led the way to the cellar door. 'Surely by now I would have noticed a secret laboratory under the stairs. Next you'll be saying that there's a nuclear reactor in the airing cupboard!'

With a *told-you-so* look on her face, Mrs Butterworth opened the door to the cellar and the three of them peered in. There were a few broken-down pieces of furniture covered with cobwebs, but nothing else. There was no evidence that Professor Middlemass's machine had ever been there.

And much to Megabyte's dismay, there wasn't even a nuclear reactor in the airing cupboard.

'It's exactly what happened at Lucy's place,' said Adam after they had left the house. 'Who are those people?'

'Imposters obviously,' said Megabyte.

'But why would somebody go to all that trouble?' asked Ami. 'What could they be hiding?'

'I just hope Lucy's still all right,' said Adam.

'We'll find her,' Megabyte reassured him. 'Eventually Mrs Butterworth will make a move. All we have to do is to follow her and bingo!'

'You guys stay here and keep an eye on Mrs Butterworth,' Adam instructed. 'I'm going back to Lucy's place to check up on this fake family and see if I can't get another lead.'

'Try not to worry, Adam,' Ami said. 'Wherever she is, I'm sure she's safe.'

'I only pray you're right!'

Chapter Seven

As Adam was teleporting to Lucy's flat, Lucy found herself being carried, bound and gagged, into a disused warehouse somewhere just off the main motorway heading out of London. It was here that Middlemass and Wilkie had driven after leaving the house in Bayswater.

Wilkie tossed her down, not particularly gently, on to a pile of sacking. 'Quit squirming, kid,' he snarled. 'Who else knows about your little visit to the house? Talk. Talk!'

'Wilkie,' said Middlemass patiently. 'It might help if you removed the gag from her mouth first, old bean.'

'What? Oh yeah, that's a good idea,' said Wilkie, and roughly ripped the gag off Lucy's mouth. Lucy considered spitting at him, but decided that to do so wouldn't be ladylike. She did it anyway.

'What happened to those photos you took?' Wilkie demanded. 'Who did you tell?'

'I don't know what you're talking about,' Lucy lied.

'Sure you do,' Wilkie sneered. 'You were taking photos back at the house. But when I tailed you back to your flat there was no film in the camera. What did you do with the film?'

'Eat socks, buster,' Lucy said. 'You don't frighten me!'

'Listen, sister. I want you to talk, and you are going to talk.'

Lucy glowered at him, unimpressed. 'Ah, you want me to talk to you 'cause you're lonely, is that it? Let's see: what shall we talk about? How do you reckon the Rams are going to do this season? You taking a vacation this year? What is the "in" resort for stressed-out thugs and hoodlums?'

'Will you just shut up and talk?'

'"Shut up and talk"?' Lucy mocked. 'You don't ask for much.'

'OK, that's it! No more pussyfooting around!' He opened up his jacket. In the inside pocket, where other people might keep their pens, Wilkie always carried two enormous syringes. He took one out and injected Lucy with it, promising, 'This is going to hurt you more than it's going to hurt me.' As the serum entered her bloodstream Lucy's eyes glazed over.

'It's a truth serum,' he explained casually to Middlemass. 'In a few seconds she'll be singing like Pavarotti's canary!' He turned back to Lucy. 'OK, sister: what did you do with those pictures?'

'Roll of film . . . Mr Bishop's office . . .' came Lucy's drugged response.

'What office? Where?' demanded Wilkie.

'Dropped it in the letter box . . . Marked "Urgent for Mr Bishop" . . . The *Recorder* . . . Craven Street . . .'

Wilkie looked smugly at Middlemass who asked: 'What do we do now?'

Wilkie sighed. 'You know, for a Grade A genius you're kinda dumb – and I should know! Now we go get the film and plug up the little security leak that's been dripping away like a busted faucet. You got any questions?'

'Just one,' said Middlemass, who had been feeling distinctly queasy after the high-speed journey from Bayswater to the warehouse. 'May I do the driving this time?'

Megabyte and Ami had to wait over an hour in the side-street in Bayswater before Mrs Butterworth left the house. They started to stalk her at a discreet distance, always keeping twenty or so paces behind. When she reached the main road she hailed a taxi and climbed in.

'Shoot! We're going to lose her now!' said Megabyte. 'We'll never find out where she's going to or who she's working for.'

'Oh yes we will,' Ami said, and waved frantically at another passing taxi. The cab pulled up and asked

Megabyte where he wanted him to take them. However, before Megabyte could say a word, Ami had pushed forwards.

'Let me do this. It's something I've always wanted to do,' she said and turned to the cabbie. 'Driver – follow that cab!'

A twenty-minute chase followed, as Megabyte and Ami's cab driver tailed Mrs Butterworth through the busy London traffic. Megabyte and Ami were frantic with worry. The traffic lights seemed always to be against them, and at least three times they thought they had lost the old lady for good.

Finally Mrs Butterworth's cab pulled up outside a seedy-looking office deep in the heart of Soho. She paid off the driver and then, checking that no one was watching, made her way into the building.

Megabyte and Ami jumped out of their own cab (much to the distress of the driver, who had been enjoying himself enormously imagining that he was in some sort of detective movie). They walked up to the tarnished brass plate by the main door and read it: Quentin D'Arcy. Theatrical Agent and Impressario.

They both exchanged puzzled looks and entered the building.

A set of rickety stairs led up to a pair of offices which were even seedier than the outside of the building if that was at all possible. Old theatrical posters decorated the wall, as well as faded black-and-white photographs of a dandyish and flamboyant man posing with men and women whose look of exaggerated self-importance made Megabyte and Ami decide that they must have been stars. Neither of them recognised any of them, which seemed to indicate that the Quentin D'Arcy Theatrical Agency had obviously seen much better days.

Mrs Butterworth was nowhere to be seen, but there was an adjoining office, and Megabyte and Ami put their ears to the door and listened.

'I am a professional actress, Mr D'Arcy,' boomed Mrs Butterworth's imperious voice. 'I played my role to perfection, and, though I say it myself, it was an artistic triumph.'

'Bravo!' came a reedy and slightly effeminate voice, which Megabyte and Ami correctly presumed belonged to D'Arcy. 'I knew you could carry it off. It sounds as though it all went swimmingly well. So what seems to be the problem?'

'I want me dosh!'

'Ah yes . . .' said D'Arcy in the cagey voice he always used when it came down to discussing money. 'Well, Mrs B, there's good news and then there's bad news . . .'

'I knew it!'

'I have your money right here on my desk,' he said. 'In fact they paid up in advance. I just haven't managed to toddle off to the bank to cash it yet.'

'Quentin D'Arcy, you have the scruples of a delinquent dung-beetle!'

'Why, thank you, Mrs B.' It was the nicest thing anyone had said to the jaded old theatrical agent in years.

'And if I don't get my money within the next twenty-four hours I shall be forced to change my representation!'

Back in the other office, Megabyte and Ami communicated telepathically with each other so as not to be overheard by D'Arcy and Butterworth.

– *We've got to look at that cheque,* Ami told him. *That's the only way we'll be able to find out who's behind this whole set-up.*

– *But how?* asked Megabyte. *Watch it! They're coming out!*

Megabyte and Ami quickly moved away from the door and sat down on a threadbare couch as D'Arcy showed Mrs Butterworth out. They hid their faces behind copies of *Variety* and *The Stage* so that she wouldn't recognise them.

Once she had gone, D'Arcy regarded the two newcomers. 'You must be here to audition for the new pimple cream commercial,' he said, ignoring Megabyte's look of indignation – he hadn't had a new zit for almost three months now! 'You're early. Wait five minutes and then come in and do your stuff.'

'Great,' said Ami, after D'Arcy had left them. 'He thinks we're here to audition! What do we do now!'

Megabyte smiled. 'There's only one thing we can do,' he said and stood up. With a theatrical flourish that would have been worthy of any top-class actor, he marched into D'Arcy's office.

Megabyte's theatrical flourishes may have been good, but if Shakespeare were alive today he would have been turning in his grave at Megabyte's acting abilities. It took him only two minutes, and approximately ten misquotes from several of the Bard's greatest plays, to convince D'Arcy that the red-headed American was probably the worst actor he had ever seen in his life.

Megabyte did, however, snatch a glimpse at the cheque on D'Arcy's desk, and, as he left the building with D'Arcy's cries of 'You untalented buffoon!' still ringing in his ears, he told Ami who had drawn it.

'It was a company called Triple-C,' he said, and wondered why the name rang a bell with him.

'Great!' said Ami. 'All we have to do now is to find out who they are and we're laughing!'

Lucy's flat was empty, its walls bare and its rooms cleared of all their furniture. It was a ghost flat, with nothing to show that Lucy – or indeed the fake family – had ever lived there. Adam was starting to despair of ever seeing Lucy again when the telephone rang. He picked up the receiver and answered.

'Who is that?' came the gruff voice at the other end. There was some interference on the line and Adam guessed that the call was being made from a mobile phone. 'I want to speak to Lucy Allen. This is Les Bishop.'

'Mr Bishop from the newspaper office?' Adam asked. 'I've got some bad news for you. Lucy's been kidnapped. She was on to some really big story – the story of the century, she called it . . .'

Bishop paused for a moment, puzzled. He knew the girl was enthusiastic, but calling the local dog show the story of the century was taking it all a bit too far even for her. But the obvious concern in Adam's voice made him realise that something was seriously wrong.

'Lucy sent me a roll of film,' he told Adam. 'Or rather she posted it through the *Recorder*'s letter box, marking the package for my urgent attention. When my secretary, Annette, found it, she had it sent up by bike to me this morning. It must be something pretty important – it could be a clue to her disappearance . . .'

'It has to be,' said Adam and then frowned. Was it his imagination or could he hear the roar of thunder in the background? 'Mr Bishop, are you all right? Mr Bishop?'

Les Bishop banged his mobile phone, his usual method of dealing with any technical malfunction. The line had turned crackly, as though affected by some electrical discharge.

And then the sky turned dark. It began to rain, first

a few drops and then more, until it was coming down in sheets. He looked across the stream where he had been fishing; a van was parked over there and two men were standing, watching him. One of them was an oily-looking weasel dressed in a posh suit; the other an older man wearing a white lab coat. The older geezer was holding some weird sort of gizmo like the satellite dish Bishop had on the wall of his house.

Both men were perfectly dry.

Bishop now was soaking wet.

A bolt of lightning cracked down from the sky, almost hitting him. Bishop jumped away, lost his balance, and fell head-first into the stream. A vicious gale blew up, churning the water, and Bishop felt himself going under for the first time.

And then a hand appeared seemingly from out of nowhere and grabbed his arm, pulling him out of the water and on to the river bank. Bishop looked up, breathless, to see Adam smiling down at him.

On the other bank Wilkie growled, and turned to Middlemass, who was aiming the saucer-shaped component of his weather machine at the sky directly above Adam and Bishop.

'It's one of those mangy maggots again. Crank the machine up!'

Already the sky was clearing, and the wind had quietened down to little more than a gentle and innocuous breeze. By the time Adam had helped the newspaper editor to his feet, the sun was shining again.

'No can do, old bean,' Middlemass said. 'The battery needs recharging, y'see.'

'Of all the stupid – ' Wilkie said despairingly. 'Get that thing back into the truck then!'

'A little "please" wouldn't hurt, you know,' Middlemass said petulantly.

'No, but a slap around the head would,' Wilkie threatened. 'Pack the machine up!'

Across the river Adam was making sure that Bishop was all right. The newspaper editor, on the other hand, was wondering just how Adam had appeared out of nowhere to save him when only twenty seconds before the boy had been a hundred miles away in West London.

However, he had no time to give in to his journalistic instincts and ask Adam for an exclusive interview, for Wilkie and Middlemass had loaded up their van, crossed the river and were heading at top speed – straight for them.

Bishop cried out, in surprise – there was nowhere to run. He shut his eyes, preparing for the inevitable impact –

– and when he opened them discovered that he was sitting on the branch of an oak tree some ten feet above the speeding vehicle, teleported up there out of harm's way by Adam. Sitting next to him on the branch, Adam grinned.

'I fell asleep, didn't I?' Bishop asked and looked warily down at the ground; it looked an uncomfortably long way down. 'This is all a dream, isn't it?'

Adam shook his head. 'I'm a friend of Lucy's,' he said, and glanced over at the truck which was now driving off into the distance. 'She's been kidnapped by those guys who just tried to kill you.'

For a second, Bishop's journalistic training made him forget that he was sitting on the branch of a tree having just been zapped up there by a teenager who had appeared out of thin air. He felt in the pocket of his anorak for the film that Lucy had sent him.

'Then she must be on to something really big,' he decided. 'We'd better get back to the office and develop this.'

'Hi, guys!'

Megabyte had blinked into existence on the branch next to them, and as Bishop turned round he lost his balance and fell crashing to the ground. It was then that he knew that he definitely wasn't dreaming.

'Well, that's one way to get down, I suppose,' said Megabyte coolly.

Chapter Eight

'Nothing! Absolutely nothing!' cried Ami and threw up her hands in desperation. She'd been sitting at her study desk for hours working at her computer and trawling through the Internet, trying to find some clue to the whereabouts of the Triple-C Corporation. The annoying thing was that the name seemed so familiar to her; Megabyte had said exactly the same before he had teleported off to see Adam.

Mrs Jackson came up and placed a sympathetic hand on her daughter's shoulder. 'Ami, don't you think it would be much more sensible if you called the police?' she asked, sensibly. Ami shook her head.

'They'd never take us seriously, Mum,' she said. 'We don't have any proof that Lucy has been kidnapped. We don't have any proof of anything. And that's why I've got to come up with something and come up with it fast.'

Mrs Jackson looked at the clock by Ami's bedside. It was 7.45 in the morning. Ami had been working all through the night.

'You can't keep going without sleep,' she said. 'Everybody needs sleep – even the Tomorrow People.'

'I have to find out what this Triple-C means if it kills me!' Ami insisted.

'Look, if you won't sleep come downstairs and have some breakfast,' her mother suggested, and Ami gave a weak smile and agreed.

'I'll just have a coffee,' she said, and followed her mother into the kitchen.

'I could do you a nice boiled egg,' Mrs Jackson suggested. 'Or maybe you'd like some cereal? Or muesli? Or what about these things?'

She took down a pack of Colonel Cobb's Corn Crinkles from the shelf, but Ami shook her head. She couldn't eat one of those loathsome corn crinkles if her life depended on it. On the front of the box beamed the smiling ruddy-cheeked face of Colonel Cobb himself: a rotund and jolly man with a bushy beard, wearing an enormous ten-gallon hat. *And what's he got to look so cheerful and smug about anyway?* Ami thought viciously.

'Mum, can you leave it out please?' Ami pleaded. 'I'm not hungry, and – of course, that's it!'

'That's what?' Mrs Jackson had no idea what Ami was talking about. Ami didn't help matters when she told her mother to look at the front of the corn crinkles box.

'Look there!' said Ami, and pointed to some small

type just below the Colonel's smiling face. She read out the three words: 'The Cobb Cereal Corporation – Triple C!'

She had tracked down the men behind Lucy's kidnapping!

Adam, Megabyte and Bishop had reached London earlier that morning (Bishop had insisted on driving down rather than being teleported there), and the first thing they did was to send Lucy's film off to the lab boys for developing.

'It's some sort of weather machine,' Adam said when the photographs had come back from the dark room. Lucy had taken some excellent black-and-whites of the rain clouds, snowstorms and lightning flashes that Professor Middlemass had created in the cellar of the West London house.

'It's incredible,' agreed Bishop. 'Absolutely unbelievable!'

'You'd better believe it, Mr B,' Adam said. 'Because whoever these guys are they're not going to let anybody stand in their way.'

There was a tapping at the door to Bishop's office and a cleaning lady popped her head round. She was doing her rounds, she told them, and would only be a minute. Bishop waved her in and continued to examine the photos.

'What do you think they're going to do with this thing?' Megabyte asked, and moved away to let the cleaning lady clean under Bishop's desk with her feather duster. On her right hand she wore a large signet ring, he noticed.

'Whatever it is they're certainly not doing it for fun,' said Bishop. 'We've all had experience of how deadly this machine can be.'

'If a mad man got in control of the weather the whole world could be at risk,' Adam said and shuddered: it was a scary prospect.

He took a closer look at one of the photographs. There was a very good image of Middlemass operating the controls of the weather machine.

'At least we know what one of them looks like,' he said as the cleaning lady finished her chores and left the office, making sure the door was closed securely behind her.

'It's a shame we can't get a good look at the other guy,' said Megabyte and shuffled through the photographs.

In each and every one of them Wilkie was turned away from the camera or his face was obscured by a piece of equipment. In fact his only visible distinguishing feature was the large signet ring he wore on his right hand.

'The ring!' cried Adam. 'The cleaning lady!'

A flash of understanding passed between Adam and Megabyte. Wilkie had infiltrated the office disguised as the cleaning lady!

'Oh boy, are we ever in trouble!' Megabyte said.

He started to rifle through the files on the top of Bishop's shelves; Adam picked up the newspaper man's in-tray and upturned it, sending unread reports and letters scattering onto the floor.

'Get searching, Mr B!' Megabyte cried.

'What are we searching for?' he asked.

'You'll know it when you find it,' said Adam.

Bishop looked under his desk. Hidden underneath it was a small timer and a stick of gelignite. He had a very bad feeling about this.

The timer was reading three seconds. Two seconds.

'I think I've found it!' Bishop said.

One second.

A massive explosion ripped through the offices of the *Recorder*, sending splinters of glass flying in all directions. A huge cloud of black and evil-smelling smoke billowed out of the window.

Down in the street Wilkie, still dragged up as a cleaning lady, chuckled into his mobile phone.

'The business went with a bang, Professor,' he reported. 'There's no way those little punks are ever going to bother us again. Once you do in the girl we'll have covered our tracks completely!'

Still chuckling, and still in his cleaning lady's outfit, Wilkie minced off to his waiting van. So full of himself and his murderous triumph was he that he failed to see Adam and Megabyte materialize in the street, with a startled Bishop in tow. Bishop shook his head and sighed.

'You know something?' he said. 'I didn't realise just how boring my life was until I met you blokes.'

Middlemass had hated the idea of killing ever since his baby sister had flushed his goldfish down the toilet bowl when he was six years old. But a million dollars was a million dollars, he reminded himself, as he stalked towards Lucy with a gun in his hand.

His heart missed a beat when he reached the corner of the warehouse where they had left the girl. She had gone.

'Where are you?' he called out in the darkness. 'Come on, now, don't muck about! I'm not going to hurt you!'

Oh yeah, . creep! Lucy thought as she watched Middlemass from behind a pile of discarded crates. There were some shards of broken glass on the ground by the crates, and she was already awkwardly cutting at her bonds with one of them. She wasn't too concerned about Middlemass – he was about as threatening as a comatose tortoise, she realised, even with a Colt .45 in his hand – but it was essential that she free herself before Wilkie got back. If he caught her trying to make a run for it, well, the guy had 'Serious Serial Killer' written all over him, and he'd no doubt take the greatest pleasure in bumping her off in the slowest and most painful way he knew . . .

'Hi, guys, what's happening?' asked Ami as she teleported in front of Adam, Megabyte and Bishop, causing the latter to jump out of his skin in surprise and make him wish for a nerve-steadying glass of the finest malt whisky.

'You just missed the fireworks,' quipped Megabyte, and nodded up at the flames issuing from the third-floor window. 'Now that we know about the weather machine they're going to try even harder to wipe us out.'

'Did you have any luck?' Adam asked her.

'I struck gold!' Ami boasted. 'The name on that cheque – Triple-C – that's the Cobb Cereal Corporation.'

'That company that makes those disgusting corn crinkles?' Megabyte said disbelievingly. 'Get outta here!'

'I know it sounds crazy, but it's true,' Ami said. 'Their main office is in Florida.'

'Look, what would a guy who makes cornflakes have to do with all this stuff?' asked Megabyte.

'Have you got any better ideas, hot shot?'

'Look, just cool it, you two, will you?' said Adam, and then noticed a commotion by the police cars which had driven up to investigate the cause of the explosion. Lucy was there arguing with the cops, insisting that she be allowed past their cordon to see Adam. Adam ran up to her and kissed her on the cheek, and the police let her through.

'Holy Toledo, what happened here?' she asked, and pointed to the offices of the *Recorder*.

'The cleaning lady,' Megabyte said nonchalantly. 'You just can't get good staff these days.'

Adam introduced Lucy to Megabyte and Ami. 'Where did they take you?' he asked.

'A warehouse near the motorway,' she said. 'Not too far out of town.'

'Do you remember how to get there?' Adam asked.

'*Puh-leease!* I'm a journalist – it's part of my job!'

Adam turned to his two fellow Tomorrow People. 'OK, here's what we do. There's no point in all of us sticking together. So you guys go off to Florida to check out this Cobb Corporation. And Lucy and I will go back to the warehouse.'

'Hey, wait a minute, you guys,' Lucy said to Megabyte and Ami. 'Florida's a long way from here and you're going to need big bucks for the plane tickets. How are you going to get there?'

Megabyte smiled at Adam. 'Well, buddy, are you going to tell her or shall I?'

Chapter Nine

Colonel Cobb, one of the world's one hundred richest men, leant back in his plush leather chair, took a sip of his whisky (specially imported at enormous expense from the Scottish Highlands) and congratulated his henchman, Wilkie, on a job well done.

'Well, that's the end of those meddling muskrats, eh?' he said and grinned into the receiver of his mobile phone. 'So all the loose ends are tied up and everything's Jim Dandy now!' He frowned when he heard the news of Lucy's escape. 'For God's sake, Wilkie, you've got more loose ends than my granny's knitting basket! Listen up, boy, we ain't got no more time to chase our tails. Operation Monsoon has got to go into action tonight. So you just get up your little backside and move it, boy! Hustle, boy, hustle!'

The Colonel slammed the phone down. He was surrounded by incompetents! Angrily he stood up and crossed over to the breakfast bar of his penthouse where, no matter what time of day or night it was, there was always an enormous bowl of Cobb's Crinkles laid out for him. He chomped thoughtfully on them – they sure were the finest breakfast vittles he had ever tasted in his life. Colonel Cobb was tired of being just one of the hundred richest men in the world; that was no longer enough for him. He wanted to be the tops, the peak, wealthier than all his fellow billionaires put together.

And when Operation Monsoon was put into effect he would be just that!

'So where do we start?' Megabyte asked as soon as he and Ami had teleported into the lobby of Cobb Towers, the worldwide headquarters of the Cobb Cereal Corporation in Florida. Their arrival had gone unnoticed so far, mainly because security had their eyes on a party of interested tourists who were being given a conducted tour of the building, but he knew that it was only a matter of time before one of the guards came up to them and demanded some form of ID.

'I reckon we should start at the very top,' Ami decided.

'Colonel Cobb himself?'

'Why not?' she asked.

'Are you kidding? That's guy's got more security than the President!' Megabyte said, and then urgently grabbed Ami's arm. One of the security guards was eyeing them up suspiciously. Thinking speedily, Ami and Megabyte walked up to the group of mainly Japanese and American tourists and tagged along with them.

A quarter of an hour later, after a potted history of the Corporation from their tour guide, an empty-headed bimbo called Tammi, Ami and Megabyte were bored to death. However, when Tammi halted briefly by an elevator door they perked up considerably.

'Now this is really something rather special,' said Tammi in a voice that was so squeaky-clean that Megabyte bet it could wash the grease off his mother's dirty pots and pans. 'This is the actual private elevator used by the great Colonel Cobb himself to take him directly up to his penthouse at the top of the tower.' She indicated a digital keyboard at the side of the elevator door. 'Only the Colonel knows the secret security code . . .'

Tammi moved her group on, but Megabyte and Ami stayed behind. Megabyte grinned and passed his hand over the keyboard. Lights flashed and tumblers clicked, and as if by magic (it was, in fact, psychokinesis) the elevator door slid open. Giving each other the thumbs-up sign, they both entered the elevator, which whisked them up to the top floor so fast that Megabyte considered pressing the 'down' button again just so he could retrieve his stomach.

The doors slid open again when it reached the top floor, and Ami and Megabyte stepped out into the plush penthouse of the hundredth richest man in the world.

Never had they seen such luxury before. Their feet

sank into carpets so soft that it seemed as though they were walking on air. The walls were hung with expensive-looking paintings, including a Van Gogh which Ami remembered having been stolen from an important American art gallery some years before. The entire room was dominated by an enormous mahogany desk, and Ami went over to it. A box, about the shape and size of a businessman's briefcase, was on the top of the desk, and Ami opened it up. Inside the box was an array of buttons and switches, and she flicked one. There was a whirring behind her and she turned to see two panels in the wall slide apart to reveal a computer screen.

'Come and have a look at this, Megabyte,' she said. 'What's this got to do with making cornflakes?'

Megabyte joined her by the desk and looked at the screen. Displayed on it was a computer-generated full-colour map of the globe. Strange lights and lines criss-crossed its surface, and they moved nearer for a closer look.

'Well, I'll be danged! What in tarnation are you two doing here?'

They both spun round. Colonel Cobb, dressed in an expensive white suit and wearing a ten-gallon hat (just like on the cornflake packets), had crept up behind them as silently as a wild cat hunting its prey. He was leaning on an elaborate walking cane and his podgy fingers tapped impatiently on its metal handle. There was an evil, threatening look in his beady little eyes as he stared at them.

'Well, I'll be horn-smockled,' he said in his distinctive Southern burr. His voice was gruff and menacing, striking fear into both their hearts.

'Er, we were with the tour party downstairs,' Ami said, and gulped as the Colonel took a step towards her. There was something dangerous about this man, she realised, something evil. 'We got lost . . .'

'Yeah,' agreed Megabyte. 'We must have taken the wrong elevator.'

The Colonel didn't say anything, but it was obvious that Megabyte and Ami weren't fooling him for one second. All three of them knew that the only way up into his penthouse suite was if someone knew, or at the very least could crack, the security code; which meant that anyone who took the elevator to the top floor of Cobb Towers did so deliberately.

'We're terribly sorry if we disturbed you, sir,' Ami said, and froze as the Colonel reached into his inside pocket to take out what she presumed was going to be a gun. She tensed, preparing to teleport away, and then relaxed as the Colonel presented each of them with a tiny complimentary box of Corn Crinkles with all the affected cheeriness of Santa dishing out presents in his grotto at Christmas time.

'Do you kids really like my Corn Crinkles?' he asked, and his voice was no longer menacing, but reminded the two of them of any number of kindly old uncles, eager to please.

'I *love* them!' lied Ami.

'Yeah, me too!' said Megabyte. 'Only the other week I bought two packs.'

'But do you really like them?' the Colonel enquired.

'Absolutely my favourite!' enthused Megabyte.

The Colonel broke into a huge smile. 'Well, then I'm mighty pleased to hear that. I'm always glad to meet folks who appreciate my product,' he chortled, and nodded to the two cereal packets which he had given to Ami and Megabyte. 'You see, I don't just put cereal in them boxes – '

You got that one right, thought Megabyte. *They taste like something you wouldn't even give to the dog.*

'No, siree,' the Colonel continued. 'I put a little bit of me into each and every box!'

Megabyte exchanged a nervous look with Ami; he was getting the tiniest suspicion that the Colonel was a hundred per cent and irretrievably round the good old bend.

'Well, we'd better be going now,' he said, and started edging towards the door. 'We're sorry if we disturbed you, sir.'

'No disturbance at all, my children,' the Colonel said effusively and led them both to the elevator. He punched out the special security code with the tip of his cane and the door sighed open. 'Now you kids all have a nice day, y'hear?'

After the elevator door had slid shut on the two

Tomorrow People the Colonel marched briskly over to his desk. He flipped open the lid of the control box and flicked a switch.

Megabyte and Ami were such charming, delightful kids and as sweet as the mint juleps his dear old sainted mama used to make way back home on the plantation in good ole Alabama. It was such a shame that he was going to have to kill them.

When the elevator door had closed on the Colonel, and the elevator began its descent, Ami and Megabyte breathed a sigh of relief.

'I wouldn't like to meet that guy in a dark alley!' Megabyte said. In spite of all the Colonel's affected bonhomie, Megabyte would have trusted the evil Doctor Culex's killer mosquitoes more than the jovial cornflake tycoon.

'He did seem a bit weird,' Ami agreed.

'A bit? The guy was totally crazy!'

'Do you think he suspected anything?'

'No,' came Megabyte's confident reply, and then he glanced up to a grille in the top of the elevator. It was starting to emit thick and noxious gas.

Megabyte didn't have time to shout out a warning to Ami, let alone to teleport. They breathed in the gas, which scorched both their lungs with its almost unbearable acidity. The world began to spin sickeningly around them, and then suddenly everything went black.

Chapter Ten

Back in London it had been a relatively simple matter for Lucy and Adam to find the warehouse in which she had been held. It had been even simpler to break into the building, although Lucy wished she could open locks as quickly and effectively as Adam. In the movies she'd seen, breaking and entry usually required bunches of skeleton keys, and, when all else failed, several tons of explosives; all Adam did was to pass his hand over the locked door and tumblers clicked into place and the door swung open apparently of its own accord. She nodded approvingly: if the boy ever decided to be a magician he'd probably make a fortune on the TV.

However, an enormous disappointment was awaiting them when they stepped into the warehouse. Apart from three deserted vehicles – a motorcycle, Wilkie's van (from which he had removed the radio, presumably on the assumption that even no-good hoodlums like him couldn't trust anyone these days), and a large van with the smiling face of Colonel Cobb emblazoned on its side – the warehouse was empty. There was no sign of Middlemass and Wilkie. For a moment Adam half expected a little old security guard to totter out of the shadows to tell them that he'd been standing guard there for twenty-odd years and he'd never seen anyone enter or leave the building. It would be exactly the same sort of trick that had been played on them at the big house in Bayswater and at Lucy's flat.

'We're too late,' he said despairingly. 'They've gone.'

Lucy sat down on an upturned packing crate. 'You never know, they might come back.'

'What for?' Adam asked, adding sarcastically: 'Maybe one of them left their toothbrush behind.'

'We haven't checked the truck yet,' Lucy said, and walked over to it. She grimaced at the smiling face of Colonel Cobb on the side: he looked a particularly sneaky customer.

Adam joined her and together they opened the back of the truck. It was filled with boxes of Colonel Cobb's Corn Crinkles. Adam sighed. What else did they expect to find inside?

'It was worth a try,' Lucy said.

'I'm going to contact Ami and Megabyte,' Adam decided. 'I'll try and find out what's happened.'

'But they're in Florida,' Lucy said sensibly, and then remembered who she was talking to. When it came to Adam, Ami and Megabyte, she was starting to realise that sensible didn't really come into it. 'Don't tell me – let me guess. You can contact them telepathically.'

'Got it in one!'

'Is there anything you guys can't do?' she asked.

Adam had to think about that one. After several moments he nodded. 'I was never too hot with a yo-yo,' he joked, and then closed his eyes, sending his thoughts out over the Atlantic Ocean to Ami and Megabyte.

When he opened his eyes there was a worried look in them. 'There's nothing,' he said. 'Just a dark empty nothing.'

'What does it mean?' asked Lucy, concerned at the urgency in his voice.

'It means trouble,' Adam said. 'If I can't get through to them it means that something's happened to them. They need me!'

'Let me come,' Lucy pleaded, but Adam shook his head. 'I can help,' she insisted.

'No – it's too dangerous,' Adam said. 'You've been through enough already and I don't want to see you hurt. Just go back to town. You'll be safe there.'

'But Adam!'

'Please?' Adam said, and looked imploringly at her with puppy-dog eyes. 'Pretty Please? Pretty Please with Sugar?'

Lucy gave in – a little too easily, thought Adam. 'OK, you sweet-talked me into it. I'll go home!'

'Thanks,' Adam said, and vanished in a flash of energy.

Now that sure was a pretty impressive way to go, Lucy told herself, as the last traces of psychic energy faded away. She hoped Adam had fallen for her promise and believed that she was really going home. Heck, she was a journalist and here was the biggest scoop of the century! How could she possibly go home and sit there twiddling her thumbs while Adam and his friends had all the fun.

She looked thoughtfully around the deserted warehouse, trying to find a clue, a lead – anything which might lead her to Middlemass and Wilkie.

Think! she scolded herself. *What would Lois Lane do in this position?*

In the basement of Cobb Towers stubby fingers tapped out the security code and the door to the Colonel's private elevator slid open to reveal Ami and Megabyte slumped unconscious on the floor.

Twitch and Beefy, two of the Colonel's body-guards with the intelligence of gorillas and the muscles and looks to match, lifted the two Tomorrow People up and carried them over to another set of elevator doors. Twitch took a special key out of the pockets of his overalls and opened the door.

The door led to the bottom of the elevator shaft. Twenty storeys above, the staff elevator was making its slow descent; Twitch knew that Tammi was about to take her tourist group on a guided tour of the oil-powered boilers in the basement. He calculated that it would take a little less than a minute for it to reach the bottom of the shaft. The two thugs laid the unconscious Ami and Megabyte in the shaft, directly underneath the rapidly approaching lift.

They stood back and locked the elevator door: even if Ami and Megabyte did wake up from their drug-induced sleep in time there would be no way that they could escape from the shaft before the elevator crushed them to a pulp.

'You like magic tricks, don't you, Beefy?' Twitch asked his colleague.

Beefy grunted.

'Well, keep watching,' Twitch said. 'Using only an ordinary elevator I'm going to show you how you can turn children into chopped liver?'

Seconds after Twitch had locked the shaft door, Ami came to. She looked around in the darkness, wondering where she was, trying to remember what had happened to her. By her side Megabyte was still unconscious. She was dimly aware of a whirring sound somewhere close above her. She looked up, squinting to try and see in the darkness of the elevator shaft. A light breeze fanned across her face, as the whirring noise got louder and louder. It was only then she realised that the elevator was headed straight for her. It was only four feet away from her now. Three feet.

Two feet.

Ami grabbed Megabyte in the darkness and tried to teleport. Nothing happened. Whether it was the after-effects of the drug that was stopping her or the fear she felt, she didn't know. All she knew was that several tons of metal were about to crush her and Megabyte to death in moments . . .

– *Adam!* she screamed inside her head. *Adam! Adam! Adam!*

Adam had been wandering through the corridors of Cobb Towers for almost half an hour, evading the security guards and searching for Ami and Megabyte. By rights, they should have left some sort of psychic trace behind them, making it possible for him to home in on them; but there was nothing. Which meant one of only two things, he realised. Either Ami and Megabyte had left the building a long time ago, or – well, he preferred not to think of the alternative.

Finally giving up, he decided to return home to Lucy, perhaps Ami and Megabyte had already teleported back there. Whatever had happened, he knew there was little he could do where he was. He sneaked behind a large potted palm and prepared to teleport.

– *Adam! Adam! Adam!*

'Ami?'

Adam sent his thoughts out through Cobb Towers

until his mind met with Ami's. The girl was terrified and not thinking straight, and all he received was a garbled jumble of half-formed thoughts and fears. He concentrated hard, entering Ami's mind, sifting through it and sorting out the confusion. He received two images: an elevator pressing down on Ami, and a sickening mess of splintered bones and steaming flesh – Ami and Megabyte's fate if he didn't act quickly.

Faster almost than thought, Adam teleported inside the elevator, which was carrying Tammi's tourists down to the basement and bringing almost certain death to his two friends. Ignoring the screams of surprise from the tourists as he appeared among them, he reached out for the control pad on the elevator wall and jabbed the button marked 'Emergency Stop'.

With a stomach-churning jolt, the elevator came to a halt. Adam sent his mind out to Ami and Megabyte: he had stopped the elevator with only inches to spare.

He gave the tourists in the elevator a sheepish grin. 'Sorry about this, folks,' he said as he teleported away. 'Have a nice day!'

Chapter Eleven

'Guys, does the phrase "Walking into the Lion's Den" suddenly seem very appropriate here?' Megabyte asked as he, Adam, and Ami teleported into Colonel Cobb's penthouse suite.

After Adam had stopped the lift, Ami had managed to teleport herself and Megabyte back to London. When the two of them had recovered, Adam had held a council of war. None of them knew exactly what Colonel Cobb was planning or why he was so interested in Professor Middlemass's weather machine, but they knew that it was important enough for him to want to kill them. Megabyte protested that this was the best reason he'd heard all week for staying away from Cobb Towers for the rest of their lives, but Adam had insisted that they all return to uncover the Colonel's plans.

'Don't worry, Megabyte, it'll be OK,' Adam said – not convincingly enough for Megabyte's liking.

'These guys aren't so clever,' Ami said and walked over to the Colonel's desk and opened his control box

'We tracked them all the way here and they haven't managed to stop us yet. And Lucy gave them the slip.'

'I'm glad she's out of danger,' said Adam. 'She's been through quite a lot in the last couple of days. By now she should be back in London, safe and sound!'

As a Tomorrow Person Adam could teleport to any place in the world and communicate telepathically with his friends, wherever they might be in that world. The one power he didn't possess, however, was an understanding of the vagaries of the human female mind – especially when the female in question was American, seventeen years of age, and Lucy Allen in search of a scoop. If he had known her better he would have realised that Lucy was not in London, and she was definitely not safe and sound.

When Adam had left her, Lucy had stayed in the warehouse to see if she could discover anything more about Middlemass and Wilkie's dastardly plan. After a good hour's snooping she had still come up with one big fat zero apart from a grubby xeroxed map in the cabin of the truck, and was about to give up and follow Adam's advice to go home, when someone entered the warehouse. Quickly she hid behind some packing cases.

Wilkie walked into the warehouse, dragging a trolley behind him. Lucy peeked out from her hiding place and saw that the trolley was loaded with a portable generator and power stacks. What did Wilkie want with those? she wondered.

Whistling tunelessly to himself, Wilkie sauntered up to the Cobb Cereal Corporation truck and opened up the back, just as she and Adam had done. Then he took a small device out of his pocket, similar to the remote-control zapper that Lucy used on her television set back home, and aimed it at the boxes of Corn Crinkles loaded in the back of the truck.

There was a whirring of engines and the boxes slid away. Lucy gasped: she and Adam had been fooled all along. The boxes weren't boxes of cereal after all, but a false front. And concealing what? Risking discovery, she sneaked out from behind the packing crates and watched as Wilkie loaded the portable generator and power stacks into the back of the truck.

What she saw took her breath away. Concealed in the back of the truck was a compact laboratory. Banks of computers lined three of the walls, while the fourth was dominated by a map of the world – she was instantly reminded of the meteorological maps she had seen on TV during weather forecasts.

Once the stacks and generator were loaded, Wilkie closed the truck and climbed into the driver's cabin at the front. He took one final look at the warehouse – Lucy got the impression that Wilkie would never be returning here again – and drive off.

A thousand questions ran through Lucy's mind. Where was Professor Middlemass? What was the purpose of the ultra-modern laboratory hidden in the back of the truck? And where was Wilkie headed?

There was only one way to find out. A motorbike was propped up against the wall of the warehouse. She leapt on to it and roared after Wilkie.

Chapter Twelve

Annette looked sympathetically at Les Bishop. Her employer – *Correction,* she told herself, *my former employer* – looked like a broken man as he pinned a notice up on the doors of the *Recorder's* offices – or rather what was left of them after Wilkie's bomb had done its work. *Closed until further notice,* it read.

'Cheer up,' she said encouragingly. 'It might never happen.'

Bishop glared at his former assistant. 'It already has,' he said. 'It might just have escaped your notice, but my office was demolished, remember?'

'Yes, I know . . .'

'For months to come they'll be picking bits of my desk out of the North Sea!'

'You've got to get over it, Mr Bishop,' Annette advised.

'Do you realise that this is the first edition not to go to print for twenty-three years?' Bishop asked her miserably.

'Chewing away at it like a dog on an old bone isn't

going to get you anywhere,' she said. 'OK, you've had a few mishaps – your office got blown up and there's a madman out there somewhere trying to kill you.' She made it sound as though they were just normal everyday hazards of the job. 'But life goes on!'

'Not for very much longer, at this rate.'

'Stop being so negative about everything,' Annette said. 'Look at me – the paper's shut down, I'm out of work, but I'm still smiling. Until we re-open I'll just take it easy and enjoy a few weeks' paid leave.'

'Ah yes . . .' said Bishop and tried to avoid looking at Annette. 'Who said anything about paid leave?'

Annette chose to ignore this last comment. 'You know what you need?' she asked.

'Yes – a bomb-proof bunker and a bottle of whisky.'

'You need a holiday.'

'I had one of those,' Bishop said, 'and look what happened there!'

'Take a complete break. Forget about the office –' she looked around – 'well, what's left of it anyway. Just get right away from it all!'

'You're absolutely right!' Bishop said. 'I'm going to get into my car right now and you're not going to see me for dust. And Annette, if any pint-sized killer comes gunning for me – don't give him my blasted address!'

Ami flicked one of the switches on the control panel

in Cobb's penthouse to reveal the computer-generated chart on the far wall. Adam studied it carefully.

'Any one got any ideas?' he asked.

'Do I get any points for recognising that it's a map of the Earth?' Megabyte asked fliply.

Ami pointed out one of two lines which circled the planet. 'This looks like some sort of trajectory,' she guessed.

'Traj-what?'

'Trajectory. It's the path of something moving around the planet. Maybe a rocket.'

Megabyte pointed to the other line, which intersected the first line somewhere over the United Kingdom. 'What about this one?' he asked.

'That's another one that kind of criss-crosses the first one,' Ami explained breezily. 'Stop me if I'm getting too technical for you here.'

Adam shook his head: he was stumped. 'The more we find out the less we seem to know.'

'And the weirder it gets too,' agreed Ami.

Megabyte had turned his attention away from the map of the world and was looking at a pile of documents which the Colonel had left beside the control panel.

'Hey, guys, look at these!' he said excitedly, and held up a sheaf of papers, all of which bore the distinctive logo of NASA, the National Aeronautical and Space Administration.

'It's a whole bunch of NASA security stuff – ID

tags, a special pass, all made out to – ' he read the name on one of the sheets of paper – 'Mel Zimmerman, rocket scientist.'

'Why would Cobb be interested in someone from the Space Centre?' Adam asked.

'Maybe he's planning on putting a little space shuttle free gift in every Corn Crinkle box?' suggested Megabyte.

'No,' said Ami. 'But there is a shuttle launch scheduled for lift-off any day now. I read about it in the papers. It's supposed to be carrying on board some new technology that will completely revolutionize the relaying of radio, TV and telephone – some sort of new communications satellite, I think.'

'This has all to tie in with the weather machine,' said Adam.

'But how?' asked Ami.

'Zimmerman lives at 20203 Allbright Avenue,' Megabyte read the address off one of the passes. 'Let's go ask him and find out how he fits in.'

'OK,' Adam finally agreed. 'But you guys be careful!'

'What about you?' asked Ami as she and Megabyte prepared to teleport.

'I'm going to stay here and snoop around a bit more,' he said.

When Ami and Megabyte had gone he started to go through the drawers of the Colonel's desk. To his frustration there seemed to be nothing pertaining to the Colonel's plans, just a bunch of press releases, some facts and figures on cornflake production, and a personally signed letter from the President of the United States saying how much he enjoyed Colonel Cobb's Corn Crinkles.

Suddenly Adam heard the elevator door swish open and he just had time to close the world chart and hide in the shadows before the Colonel and Professor Middlemass walked into the penthouse. Middlemass was dressed in a Hawaiian shirt and a ridiculous pair of Bermuda shorts, and from the conversation he was having with the Colonel it seemed that he had just arrived off the plane from England.

'Make yourself at home, Professor Middlemass,' said the Colonel, and showed him to his second-best armchair. 'Might I offer you your choice of refreshing beverage?'

Middlemass declined: he had been airsick all during the nine-hour flight to Florida and he was still feeling a little queasy.

'I'm mighty sorry to hear that, son,' the Colonel said, and poured himself a large glass of Scotch. 'I trust your little indisposition will not affect your part in my grand plan?'

'Not at all,' Middlemass said, thinking of the million dollars he was to receive for helping the Colonel. 'I'm raring to go! The experiments have been a total success, and the test results are outstanding – stupendous even. If I say so myself, the weather machine is sheer poetry in motion.'

'Cut the poetry,' the Colonel said, suddenly all brisk and business-like. 'Is Operation Monsoon going to work or isn't it?'

'Indubitably!' Middlemass reassured him.

He reached into his briefcase and brought out a slim file which he handed to the Colonel. 'I've brought you a complete report of all the work we've done so far, together with statistical analysis.'

The Colonel grabbed the report from Middlemass, tore it up and threw the pieces into the wastepaper bin.

'Are you out of your tiny cotton-picking mind, boy?' he barked angrily. 'I said nothing – repeat, nothing – of this little escapade was to be committed to paper! You write something down and sure as eggs is eggs some beady-eyed little horny toad's going to sneak a squint at it.'

(In the shadows Adam nodded to himself: the Colonel's aversion to committing anything to paper explained the lack of any incriminating evidence in his desk drawers.)

'Now just bring me up to date yourself,' the Colonel ordered.

'Well, at about this time – ' Middlemass checked his watch – 'Wilkie should have collected the equipment and be on his way to the airport. We rendezvous with him there, proceed to the transmission site, set up the equipment, wait for the right moment – and Bob's your uncle!'

The Colonel stood up and did a little celebratory jig. 'Now you're talking!' he crowed. 'I'm as jumpy as a long-tailed cat in a room full of rocking chairs! I can see it now. Tomorrow I just turn on that little ole weather machine of yours and bring destruction and devastation a-raining down on the cornfields of central USA. All my rivals' cereal production wiped out at a stroke! But me, with my secret supplies intact, will become the new Cornflake King of the World! I shall be the Emperor of Maize, the Colonel of Kernels.' Cobb threw back his head and laughed, a long maniacal laugh which, in his hiding-place, made Adam shiver with horror.

'Nothing – and nobody – in the world can stop me now!'

Colonel Cobb was one of the richest and most powerful men on the entire planet. He was also totally and incurably insane.

Chapter Thirteen

'Now, remember you are Doctor Zimmerman,' the Colonel said as he inspected Professor Middlemass like a general reviewing his troops before a big battle. The professor was wearing the uniform of a NASA employee with the security pass on his lapel, and the ID papers the Colonel had provided him with identified him as Doctor Melvin Zimmerman. 'I'm depending on you, boy. Get this right and I'll have you to dinner. Get this wrong and I'll have you *for* dinner. Do you read me loud and clear?'

'Oh very loud, Colonel Cobb,' Middlemass said. 'And very clear.'

'You understand what you have to do, my boy?' The Colonel asked one final time. 'Because from now on the operation rests entirely on your shoulders!'

Middlemass nodded. 'I'm to penetrate NASA security,' he repeated for what seemed like the millionth time.

'With Zimmerman's ID that'll be as simple as shooting fish in a barrel,' the Colonel smiled.

'The space shuttle *Ventura* is due to launch a communications satellite today,' Middlemass continued, and took a computer panel from his jacket pocket. 'I'm to replace its guidance system with this – which will link it to our own tracking system . . .'

The Colonel beamed and gave Middlemass a hearty slap on the back. 'In exactly one hour, then, Professor, I'll meet you at the airport,' he said. 'And then – and then bring on the rains!'

'Well, this is Zimmerman's house,' Megabyte said to Ami, and he looked up at the pleasant suburban home on the outskirts of Cape Canaveral, the headquarters of NASA in East Florida. It had taken them quite a while to find the place, hidden as it was just off the road in its own private grounds. 'What do you want to do? Check out the backyard or teleport inside?'

'We'll knock on the door,' decided Ami.

'Are you sure?' gasped Megabyte, for whom the idea seemed incredibly simple and quaint.

'We'll say we're lost,' said Ami, 'and ask for directions. That way we'll get an idea of what he's like.'

Megabyte shrugged and rapped on the door. To their surprise it was already open, and, treading warily, they entered Zimmerman's house.

The house was decorated in a chintzy style and the walls adorned with framed photographs of movie stars but, apart from a parrot sitting and squawking on its perch, it was deserted. There was no sign of Zimmerman. Yet the lights were on and the TV was turned on, as though the man from NASA had just gone out for a moment.

'I've checked upstairs,' Ami said as she rejoined Megabyte in the living room. 'There's no sign of him.'

'Well obviously the guy's split,' he said. 'Let's go.'

Ami wasn't so sure. 'It's weird though, the door being open like that,' she said, and looked over at the parrot as though he might be able to tell her something.

'It's a wotsit in the closet!' the parrot squawked.

'Can it, big breath!' Megabyte snarled.

'Can it!' the parrot repeated.

'Old Mother Hubbard went to the cupboard,' the parrot continued.

'Quit that squawking!' Megabyte said. How was he supposed to think with the blasted parrot chattering on all the time?

'There's a wotsit in the closet!' the parrot repeated.

'That's it!' Megabyte decided. 'I'm going to wring its stupid neck.'

'Wait, Megabyte,' Ami said and pointed to the closet door. It was slightly ajar. She walked over and opened it. Bundled up in the bottom of the closet, bound and gagged, was a man: Zimmerman.

Megabyte shot a look at the parrot. 'OK, we all

make mistakes,' he said, and helped to free Zimmerman from his closet.

'A man's not safe in his own house!' Zimmerman said indignantly after they had untied him and removed the tape from his mouth. 'There I was, sitting here, eating potato chips and watching an old Fred Astaire movie . . .'

'What happened?' Megabyte demanded anxiously.

'Fred thought that Ginger didn't love him any more,' he said sadly.

'No! Not the movie!'

'Oh, right. . . . Well, these real big guys arrived,' he said. 'They wanted to know if I worked at the Space Centre, and then they made me hand over all my security stuff.' He sighed. 'Mother was right, you know. I should have been a dentist.'

'It all fits!' said Ami excitedly. 'They got you out of the way and stole all your stuff so they could get to the space shuttle!'

'We've got to stop the countdown!'

Zimmerman reached for the phone and tapped out the top-security number which was a direct line to NASA mission control. But it was too late. Ami pointed to the TV screen. The movie had finished and the station had switched to a news broadcast of the space shuttle *Ventura*. The three of them watched in horror as the ignition sequence ended and the shuttle began to rise into the air.

'We're too late!' Ami said and didn't even turn as

Adam appeared beside her. Zimmerman, however, jumped out of his skin.

'Adam, they've broken into NASA,' Megabyte said. 'They've done something to the shuttle. It's too late.'

'It's never too late!' Adam insisted. 'Cobb has to be stopped.'

'That's pretty difficult when we don't even know what he's doing,' Ami pointed out.

'But we do!' Adam said and told them what he had learnt when he was eavesdropping on the Colonel and Middlemass.

Ami was horrified. 'Mucking around with the weather on a scale like that could be disastrous,' she said.

'That's right,' Adam agreed. 'It could destabilize the whole eco-structure of the planet.'

'Heavy,' was Megabyte's contribution to the discussion.

'Excuse me for even daring to exist,' said Zimmerman who was feeling a little miffed that total strangers were literally appearing out of nowhere in his house, and, what was worse, ignoring him. 'Would someone please tell me what's going on?'

Ami continued to ignore him. 'So we know what they want to do but we don't know where,' she said.

'In other words we're up the Mississippi without a paddle boat,' concluded Megabyte.

'We've got one clue – the chart in Cobb's office,' Adam said. 'That's got to tell us something.'

'No, Adam,' Megabyte said. 'We all looked at that thing and what did we discover? Zilch, that's what!'

'He's right,' said Ami. 'Let's face it: none of us understands it.'

'I'm no rocket scientist,' said Megabyte and turned to Zimmerman. 'But I know a guy who is.'

Suddenly Zimmerman discovered that he was no longer being ignored.

It was mid-afternoon by the time Lucy – tired, dirty, and generally fed-up with the whole world – reached the main road. She had no idea exactly how far away from London she was as she had been pursuing Wilkie on her motorbike for the better part of the night. *Some journalist I am!* she thought as she trudged along the dusty country road. She had been feeling pretty smug about having successfully tailed Wilkie to another warehouse, somewhere to the north of London, where he had picked up some more equipment. As far as she knew he hadn't spotted her, and she was giving herself the first of many thousand pats on the back when the bike she was riding ran out of petrol. She cursed herself for being a little idiot and not checking the fuel tank when she had set off, and looked on helplessly as Wilkie steered the truck on to the motorway and in the direction of London airport. She wondered who he was going to meet there; she also wondered how in heaven's name she was going to get home.

She held out her thumb to hitch a lift and was surprised when the first car to come along stopped for her. She was even more surprised when she recognised the driver of the battered old Volvo.

'Mr Bishop!' she cried delightedly, and climbed into the passenger seat. 'Boy, you don't know just how glad I am to see you. It's a chance in a million running into you like this.'

Bishop buried his face in his hands. 'Why me?' he cried. 'What have I ever done to deserve this?'

'Mr Bishop, are you all right?' Lucy asked, full of concern.

'Of course I'm all right,' he replied sarcastically, hoping he was making it perfectly plain that he wasn't all right at all. 'Don't I look over the moon? Can't you see me dancing on air?'

'What is it, Mr B?' Lucy asked. Who was he trying to kid: she was an ace reporter after all and there was no fooling her. 'There's something wrong, isn't there?'

'Nothing at all,' he lied.

'You can tell me,' she said confidently. 'We're buddies.'

'We are, are we?' he said, and looked her directly in the eye. 'Then I will tell you. You see, it's just that a week ago I had a job. I even liked my job. I came to work, I sat at my desk, I wrote a few letters, made a few phone calls. The biggest excitement I had was breaking the lead in my pencil. And then *you* walk

107

into my life with your cock-eyed stories and your crazy friends, and bang, crash, wallop and I'm half-drowned in a river by a freak storm. I fall out of a tree, I'm nearly killed by a maniac hit-and-run driver, and I've a demented old cleaning lady blow up my office with a bomb!'

'Chin up, Mr B,' Lucy said encouragingly. 'All I need from you is one little favour. You just start driving and I'll fill you in along the way.'

'I can't believe I'm doing this again, and listening to you,' the newspaper man marvelled as he revved up the engine and started off back down the road.

'We've got to find that truck,' Lucy said. 'It's got a real head start on us, but if you put your foot down we can do it.'

'And would it be too much to ask just where I'm supposed to be driving to?' Bishop asked sarcastically, and Lucy handed him the photocopied map she had found in the cabin of Wilkie's van.

'You know the place?' she asked, indicating the spot on the map which Wilkie had marked, and Bishop nodded.

It was Battersea Power Station.

'What happened?' asked Zimmerman. 'Where am I?' Just a second before he had been in his own comfy living-room with these three weird kids. Now he was standing in a lush penthouse suite which looked out over the Florida coast.

'There's no time to explain, Doctor Zimmerman,' Adam said, after he had checked that the startled scientist was feeling all right after having been teleported into the Colonel's office.

'We really need your help,' Ami said, and ran over to the control box on the desk. 'We just need you to tell us what this chart means.' She flipped a switch and the shutters on the far end of the wall opened to reveal – not the chart showing the map of the world, but the smiling cartoon face of Colonel Cobb that was to be found on every packet of Corn Crinkles.

'You flipped the wrong switch,' Megabyte said. And then, 'Look out!'

Tiny poison-tipped darts flew out of the Colonel's open mouth and the three Tomorrow People dived to the floor, taking cover behind a sofa. Zimmerman wasn't so quick, however, and a dart struck him just above the heart. As soon as the darts had stopped firing Adam was by his side.

'Are you OK?' he asked.

'Don't panic!' said Zimmerman, and removed the dart from his chest. 'It hit my credit cards. Now is that lucky or what?'

Megabyte breathed a sigh of relief. 'You had us going for a moment, Mr Z,' he admitted.

'You don't have to worry about old miracle Melvin Zimmerman,' he bragged. 'No, siree! I can look after myself.'

Zimmerman sat down on the sofa – and right on

top of a dart. The poison on the dart's tip took its effect almost immediately, and the rocket scientist started to fall fast asleep.

'Oh no!' cried Adam, and slapped the man on the cheeks in an attempt to keep him awake. He signalled to Ami and Megabyte to help him stand Zimmerman up and move him over to the wall chart, the correct switch for which Ami had finally found.

'OK, Mr Zimmerman,' Adam said, 'it's time for you to do some work. Look at the chart.'

Zimmerman stared at the chart through misty and tired eyes. All he really wanted to do was to sleep – for a long, long time . . .

'Come on, fella!' Megabyte urged. 'Stay awake!'

'We're losing him,' said Ami, as the Colonel's sleeping drug took its full effect and Zimmerman slumped to his knees.

'We're depending on you,' Megabyte said. He and Adam picked him up again. 'Tell us what the chart means.'

Zimmerman stared at the chart. Everything was becoming very woozy for him now. 'The blue line must be the satellite trajectory,' he guessed, slurring his words.

'And the red one?' demanded Ami.

Zimmerman yawned. 'Must . . . get . . . some sleep . . .'

'No, you can sleep later,' Adam said. 'What does the red line mean?'

'It must be the new trajectory. . . . They're hijacking the satellite.'

Finally the drug took its toll on Zimmerman, and he fell to the floor, where he curled up and started snoring.

'He'll be all right once he's slept it off,' said Adam.

'The weather machine!' said Megabyte. 'If Cobb gets control of that satellite they'll be able to bounce the weather machine's power off it and create any kind of storm anywhere in the world.'

'*If* they get control,' said Ami. 'Maybe we can stop them first.'

Adam looked at where the red and the blue lines on the chart converged: England. That had to be where Cobb and Middlemass were now.

'I hate to bring you down to Earth with a bump, guys,' said Ami. 'We know it's going to happen in England but it could be anywhere. Where do we start looking? – Adam, what are you doing?'

Adam was frantically searching through the contents of Colonel Cobb's bin. 'Professor Middlemass had this file on the weather machine,' he explained. 'Cobb tore it up and threw it in here.'

Finally he found what he was looking for – and discovered that none of them could make head or tail of the complex scientific equations. Nowhere was there any mention of where in England Cobb and Middlemass were planning to put their evil plan into operation.

'Wait a minute,' said Adam, picking up the remains of a black-and-white photograph which Cobb had also torn to pieces. 'This could be it!'

They collected the pieces of torn photographs, and Megabyte assembled them. They found that they were all looking at the image of a very familiar sight indeed: a huge derelict building, whose four towers, one at each corner, made it resemble a gigantic upturned piano stool.

'It's the power station in Battersea in South London!' Ami exclaimed.

'OK, we'll have to assume that this is where they're heading,' said Adam. 'If we're right we might just be in time to stop them – if not, well, then we're in real big trouble.'

Chapter Fourteen

Night had fallen over England by the time Wilkie had picked up the Colonel and Middlemass from London airport and driven them over to Battersea Power Station. The derelict power station stood lonely and forlorn on the banks of the River Thames, its gutted interior open to the clear summer skies; but inside the van, which Wilkie had parked inside the old power station, the excitement was mounting with every second.

The Colonel could not conceal his glee as he watched the progress of the satellite on the tracking system that Middlemass had rigged up. Everything was going according to plan, and soon – very soon now – he was going to be the richest man in the history of the entire world.

'How are we doing, boy?' he asked Middlemass who was sitting hunched over a computer console.

'We're almost there,' Middlemass confirmed, and operated a touch-sensitive control. A panel in the roof of the truck opened to reveal a large aerial, which spun around for a few seconds as if searching out a signal.

Inside the truck Middlemass adjusted a few controls to align the aerial with the satellite. As soon as the satellite was directly overhead, the device would lock itself on to it, immobilising it in the depths of space, and thereby enabling them to project the energies of the weather machine on to it.

'All of my dreaming and my praying is about to come true!' the Colonel gushed.

'Amen to that, Colonel!' said Wilkie.

'I'd like to be a little old fly on that wall to see all their foolish faces as their precious crops are swallowed up in a sea of mud and devastation.'

'That'll sure sicken their chicken!' Wilkie agreed gleefully.

''Cause if they ain't got no crops then they ain't got no breakfast cereal,' said the Colonel, and banged his metal-topped walking cane on the floor as if to emphasise his point. 'And then I, Jeremiah Cobb, shall step forth and seize the crown as the King of the Cornflake World!'

'I knew you could do it, Colonel Cobb,' Wilkie said loyally.

'Why, thank you, my boy,' the Colonel said, genuinely touched. He accepted Wilkie's proffered handkerchief and dabbed at his own eyes. 'Why, I do declare that the momentousness of this occasion is making me a mite misty around the old peepers.'

'The satellite's coming into position,' Middlemass said excitedly. 'Activating interceptor – now!'

Middlemass flicked a switch and the aerial on top of the truck emitted a long, steady bolt of electromagnetic energy, which soared through the atmosphere and out into space, trapping the satellite in its powerful grasp. Soon, Middlemass realised, Operation Monsoon would be in full operation – and the million dollars that Colonel Cobb had promised him would be his!

'Look, Mr Bishop! It's started!' cried Lucy, as Bishop's car drove up to the power station. Against the blackness of the sky they could clearly see the white beam of light as it streaked up from the aerial and towards the heavens.

She leapt out of the car and started running towards the old power station. 'I've got to do something!' she cried.

'No, Lucy, you can't!' protested Bishop.

'Go get the police – and hurry.'

'I'm not leaving you here.'

'I'll be OK – I just want to stay here and watch,' she claimed.

'You won't do anything silly?'

'Who me? Get outta here. Now go!'

As Bishop drove off to the police station Lucy looked at the power station. She had never done anything silly in her life, she kept telling herself. Well, apart from spying on that house in Bayswater in the first place, getting involved with Adam and his weirdo friends and almost getting killed by a psycho who thought he was a part-time hood from a 1940s gangster movie . . .

And it has now been confirmed that there is, in fact, a serious malfunction in the Delta Three satellite launched earlier today from the Ventura *space shuttle,* the CNN news announcer reported on the Colonel's portable TV. *Speaking just moments ago, the NASA Space Centre has intimated sabotage, and the use of some kind of device to draw the satellite off-course . . .*

The Colonel switched off the TV and whooped. 'Dearie, dearie me, it seems that those poor bozoes have gone and lost their little ole satellite! Now I wonder where it could be?'

Middlemass looked up from his tracking equipment. 'We have control of the satellite. It's being directed over the cornfields now,' he informed his employer.

'Well, boys, what are we waiting for?' the Colonel asked impatiently. 'Kick that mule! Nuke them crops! It's tempest time!'

Middlemass operated a control, and a second panel in the roof of the van opened up to reveal the dish of his weather machine. It would take a few minutes for the machine to warm up, but when it did the beam of energy it produced would reflect off the captured satellite and cause untold devastation throughout America.

Operation Monsoon had begun. And – if the Tomorrow People were right – not just the American cornfields, but the whole world was in danger.

As soon as she was sure that Bishop was out of sight, Lucy had raced into the interior of the abandoned power station and headed directly for Colonel Cobb's van. This was the source of all the trouble, she realised, and all she knew was that she had somehow to stop the weather machine from being operated.

She found a heavy metal spanner on the ground and picked it up. A ladder was standing, propped up against the wall, and she lifted it up and leant it gently against the side of the van, hoping that whoever was in there would not hear her above the noise of Middlemass's interceptor device. Carefully she climbed up the side of the truck and on to its roof.

'Well, well, well, and look who we have here!'

Lucy turned around. Wilkie had followed her up the ladder and was facing her on the roof. Obviously she hadn't been quiet enough, and he had come out of the truck to investigate. He darted for her, wresting the heavy spanner from her hand.

'I'll give you one thing, babe: you're persistent,' he said. 'But persistence ain't gonna do you no good when you're dead.'

He brought the spanner crashing towards Lucy's

skull. Lucy pulled away and the spanner missed her by inches. She scrambled towards Middlemass's weather device, which was beaming up its deadly energies to the satellite in space. Any second now and it would reach full power.

Wilkie aimed the spanner at Lucy, and threw it. It missed her, and instead hit the weather device, upsetting its centre of balance. Its beam was knocked away from the space satellite. Now it pointed directly overhead. Middlemass's weather device, originally designed to disrupt the weather over middle America, started to produce climatic changes over London SW8.

There was an enormous crash of thunder and the heavens opened. Torrents of rain started to pour down on the power station, and a powerful wind blew up, making it almost impossible for Lucy and Wilkie to maintain their balance on the roof of the truck. A huge bolt of lightning seared out of the sky and struck the truck. There was an enormous explosion, and both Lucy and Wilkie were thrown off the roof by the force of the blast. They landed on the ground with a bone-jarring thud.

Inside the truck, machines exploded and computers suddenly burst into flames, showering Middlemass and the Colonel in sparks.

'What in tarnation is going on?' cried the Colonel. 'Do something, boy!'

'There's nothing I can do!' Middlemass shouted,

straining to make himself heard above the noise of the exploding machines. 'It's out of control!'

'You bumbling fool. Make it stop!'

'It's not responding. Every circuit's overloading! We have to leave!'

'You leave, you lily-livered mongrel!' the Colonel bellowed as Middlemass opened the back of the truck and leapt out. 'I don't need you anymore! I don't need nobody!'

Outside the truck Adam appeared in a flash of energy. He helped Lucy to her feet, and quickly took in the situation. It seemed that he, Ami and Megabyte had arrived just in the nick of time. He ran over to Middlemass, who had just jumped out of the truck.

'What do we have to do to stop this thing?' he cried above the howling of the wind and the ear-shattering rumbles of thunder.

'You can't!' Middlemass cried, and looked over to the truck. Smoke was billowing out of its engine, and on its roof the weather machine was spouting flames. 'It's gone too far. When this thing goes up, matey, then we're all doomed! Doomed!'

'Not if I can help it,' Adam said. He ran to the truck and leapt into the driver's cab.

'No, Adam! You can't!' cried Ami, who had guessed what Adam was planning to do.

'It's the only way!' Adam shouted, and he revved up the engine. As the truck moved off, Colonel Cobb leapt out of the back. Megabyte and Ami raced towards him.

'It's all over now, Colonel Cobb!' Megabyte cried. 'Give yourself up. It's finished.'

Through the torrents of rain, Colonel Cobb looked hated at the cursed teenagers who had thwarted his every plan. 'Finished?' he laughed, like the madman he had now proved himself to be. 'I'll show you who's finished!'

He advanced on Megabyte and Ami, brandishing his metal-topped cane like a club, ready to strike them.

Suddenly a bolt of energy shot out of the sky – whether it was a lightning flash or some residual power from the weather machine the Tomorrow People weren't quite sure. Attracted by the metal top of the Colonel's cane, which acted as an effective conductor, it streaked down into Cobb's entire body. There was a sickening stink of burning flesh, Colonel Jeremiah Cobb let out a scream of pain, and he fell, lifeless, to the floor.

'Is he dead?' Ami asked.

Megabyte bent down to examine the mad man. He was in an advanced state of shock and had suffered some nasty burns but it seemed that he would live.

'Adam!' screamed Lucy. She pointed to the far end of the power station. Adam was driving at top speed straight towards a brick wall.

There was an enormous explosion as the truck

smashed into the wall. The smell of burning rubber and the bitter stench of molten metal hung in the air. The weather machine had been destroyed, and, in the sky over Battersea Power Station, the dark storm clouds faded away. Within seconds it seemed that they had never been there at all, and the warm summer moon beamed down on Ami, Megabyte and Lucy.

Lucy walked miserably up to the remains of the truck. In the distance she could hear the sirens of the police cars which Mr Bishop had alerted. Her eyes were flooding with tears, but she made no attempt to wipe them away. In destroying Middlemass's weather machine Adam had sacrificed himself for them all, she realised. He had called himself a Tomorrow Person, she recalled; said that he and his kind were the future of the world. It was ironic that, for Adam, there would be no more future . . .

'You can't get rid of me that easily!' a familiar voice chirped up behind her.

She swung round to see Adam appear out of thin air. He had teleported away from the driver's truck a nano-second before it had hit the wall, he explained; after all, they hadn't been out for that cup of coffee yet, he reminded her, and he wasn't going to pass up a chance like that.

'And maybe now this is over we could . . .' he said awkwardly. 'I mean, do you think . . .'

'That we might see each other again?' she finished for him. 'You just try and stop me!'

Delighted, Adam took her hand and rejoined Ami and Megabyte. Mr Bishop had arrived with the police, who were already leading away Middlemass, Wilkie and a rapidly recovering Colonel Cobb.

Megabyte grinned at Bishop. 'Some scoop, huh, Mr B?'

'Well, I have to admit it's the biggest exclusive I've ever run into,' he admitted. 'And you lot with your special powers – I can't wait to . . .'

'Sorry, Mr B,' said Adam and laughed. 'You'll have to leave out that part of the story, I'm afraid.'

Ami joined in his laughter. 'Somehow I don't think the world's quite ready for the Tomorrow People yet.'

'Hey, don't worry, Mr Bishop,' Lucy said cheerfully. 'Leave it to me. I'll give you a piece that'll knock your socks off! That is, if you still want me to work for you after all this . . .'

'Of course I want you to work for me,' Bishop said hastily: there was no way he wanted Lucy to go to a rival paper with her scoop. 'In fact, when you've finished your studies there'll be a job waiting for you.'

'Wow! You're a peach, Mr Bish!' She turned to Adam, Ami and Megabyte. 'You hear that, you guys! A real-live Lois Lane!'

'Congratulations, Lucy!' said Adam, and kissed her – this time on the lips. 'I told you that you could do it!'

Lucy smiled and turned back to Bishop. 'And next time, Mr Bishop – sorry, Boss,' she corrected herself, and continued: 'I don't care what you want me to write about – dog shows, church fetes. . . . Heck, I'll even do the weather forecast!'